DRENA AND THE DUKE

The Dowager Countess of Winterton is very anxious for her beloved granddaughter Drena to marry her relative the Duc de Saulieu of Burgundy, and so they travel to his Chateau where Drena is repulsed by him, even though he seems very keen to charm her.

When Drena visits the Library to borrow some books, the Curator tells her about the secret "listening holes" which one of the more eccentric Ducs had made in the walls. By accident, Drena finds one of these in her Boudoir and to her horror overhears the Duc and his mistress plotting to marry, then kill her in a carefully arranged "accident".

Horrified, she runs away, telling her grandmother she is going to stay with some friends nearby.

Drena escapes to Fabrey, and is given sanctuary by the Priest before a stranger comes to the village. Eventually she returns with him to the Chateau de Saulieu.

How the plots of the wicked Duc finally fail are all told in this exciting story, the 496th by Barbara Cartland.

DRENA AND THE DUKE

Barbara Cartland

SEVERN HOUSE PUBLISHERS

This first world edition published in Great Britain 1992 by
SEVERN HOUSE PUBLISHERS LTD of
35 Manor Road, Wallington, Surrey SM6 0BW.
First published in the U.S.A. 1992 by
SEVERN HOUSE PUBLISHERS INC of
475 Fifth Avenue, New York, NY 10017

Copyright © 1992 by Barbara Cartland

British Library Cataloguing in Publication Data
Cartland, Barbara, *1902–*
  Drena and the Duke
  I. Title
  823.912 [F]

ISBN 0-7278-4346-X

Typeset in Linotron Sabon by
Hewer Text Composition Services, Edinburgh
Printed and bound in Great Britain by
Billing and Sons Ltd, Worcester

AUTHOR'S NOTE

I wrote this novel after my visit to Burgundy in June 1989.

Burgundy is the wine country of France, from the vineyards of which come Chablis, Chambertin, Pouilly, Pommard, and many others.

It is a mellow land of rivers and canals and has a vast store of art treasures. Indeed the days of opulence are reflected in all their Chateaux which are like Palaces.

Burgundy has more legends and more fairy-tales than anywhere else in France. There are also reminders of pre-History: Celts, Gauls, and Romans.

As soon as I enter the Province I feel the magic of it coming into my mind and it is very easy to obtain not one plot for a book, but a hundred; the beauty of France seems to speak to one from every vineyard, from every silver river and every ancient building.

ABOUT THE AUTHOR

Barbara Cartland, the world's most famous romantic novelist, who is also an historian, playwright, lecturer, political speaker and television personality, has now written over 507 books and sold over 500 million copies all over the world.

She has also had many historical works published and has written four autobiographies as well as the biographies of her mother and that of her brother, Ronald Cartland, who was the first Member of Parliament to be killed in the last war. This book has a preface by Sir Winston Churchill and has just been republished with an introduction by the late Sir Arthur Bryant.

"Love at the Helm" a novel written with the help and inspiration of the late Earl Mountbatten of Burma, Great Uncle of His Royal Highness The Prince of Wales, is being sold for the Mountbatten Memorial Trust.

She has broken the world record for the last fourteen years by writing an average of twenty-three books a year. In the Guiness Book of Records she is listed as the world's top-selling author.

Miss Cartland in 1978 sang an Album of Love Songs with the Royal Philharmonic Orchestra.

In private life Barbara Cartland, who is a Dame of Grace of the Order of St. John of Jerusalem, Chairman of the St. John Council in Hertfordshire and Deputy President of the St. John Ambulance Brigade, has fought for better conditions and salaries for Midwives and Nurses.

She championed the cause for the Elderly in 1956 invoking a Government Enquiry into the "Housing Conditions of Old People".

In 1962 she had the Law of England changed so that Local Authorities had to provide camps for their own Gypsies. This has meant that since then thousands and thousands of Gypsy children have been able to go to School which they had never been able to do in the past, as their caravans were moved every twenty-four hours by the Police.

There are now fourteen camps in Hertfordshire and Barbara Cartland has her own Romany Gypsy Camp called Barbaraville by the Gypsies.

Her designs "Decorating with Love" are being sold all over the U.S.A. and the National Home Fashions League made her, in 1981, "Woman of Achievement".

Barbara Cartland's book "Getting Older, Growing Younger" has been published in Great Britain and the U.S.A. and her fifth Cookery Book, "The Romance of Food", is now being used by the House of Commons.

In 1984 she received at Kennedy Airport, America's Bishop Wright Air Industry Award for her contribution to the development of aviation. In 1931 she and two R.A.F. Officers though of, and carried, the first aeroplane-towed glider air-mail.

During the War she was Chief Lady Welfare Officer in Bedfordshire looking after 20,000 Service men and women. She thought of having a pool of Wedding Dresses at the War Office so a Service Bride could hire a gown for the day.

She bought 1,000 secondhand gowns without coupons for the A.T.S., the W.A.A.F.s and the W.R.E.N.S. In 1945 Barbara Cartland received the Certificate of Merit from Eastern Command.

In 1964 Barbara Cartland founded the National Association for Health of which she is the President, as a front for all the Health Stores and for any product made as alternative medicine.

This has now a £500,000,000 turnover a year, with one third going in export.

In January 1988 she received "La Medaille de Vermeil de la Ville de Paris", (the Gold Medal of Paris). This is the highest award to be given by the City of Paris for ACHIEVEMENT – 25 million books sold in France.

In March 1988 Barbara Cartland was asked by the Indian Government to open their Health Resort outside Delhi. This is almost the largest Health Resort in the world.

Barbara Cartland was received with great enthusiasm by her fans, who also fêted her at a Reception in the city and she received the gift of an embossed plate from the Government.

OTHER BOOKS BY BARBARA CARTLAND

Other novels, over 500, the most recently published being:

Born of Love
The Angel and the Rake
The Queen of Hearts
The Wicked Widow
To Scotland and Love
Love and War
Love at the Ritz
The Dangerous Marriage
Good or Bad
This is Love
Seek the Stars
Running Away to Love
Look with the Heart
Safe in Paradise
Love in the Ruins
A Coronation of Love
A Duel of Jewels
The Duke is Trapped
Just a Wonderful Dream
Love and a Cheetah
The Dream and the Glory (In aid of the St. John Ambulance Brigade)

Autobiographical and Biographical:

The Isthmus Years 1919–1939
The Years of Opportunity 1939–1945
I Search for Rainbows 1945–1976
We Danced All Night 1919–1929
Ronald Cartland (With a foreword by Sir Winston Churchill)
Polly – My Wonderful Mother
I Seek the Miraculous

Historical:

Bewitching Women
The Outrageous Queen (The Story of Queen Christina of Sweden)
The Scandalous Life of King Carol
The Private Life of Charles II
The Private Life of Elizabeth, Empress of Austria
Josephine, Empress of France
Diane de Poitiers
Metternich – The Passionate Diplomat
A Year of Royal Days
Royal Jewels
Royal Eccentrics
Royal Lovers

Sociology:

You in the Home
The Fascinating Forties
Marriage for Moderns
Be Vivid, Be Vital
Love, Life and Sex
Vitamins for Vitality
Husbands and Wives
Men are Wonderful
Etiquette
The Many Facets of Love
Sex and the Teenager
The Book of Charm
Living Together
The Youth Secret
The Magic of Honey
The Book of Beauty and Health
Keep Young and Beautiful by Barbara Cartland and Elinor Glyn
Etiquette for Love and Romance
Barbara Cartland's Book of Health

Cookery:

Barbara Cartland's Health Food Cookery Book
Food for Love
Magic of Honey Cookbook
Recipes for Lovers
The Romance of Food

Editor of:

"The Common Problem" by Ronald Cartland (with a preface by the Rt. Hon. the Earl of Selborne, P.C.)
Barbara Cartland's Library of Love
                Library of Ancient Wisdom
"Written with Love". Passionate love letters selected by Barbara Cartland

Drama:

Blood Money
French Dressing

Philosophy:

Touch the Stars

Radio Operetta:

The Rose and the Violet (Music by Mark Lubbock) Performed in 1942.

Radio Plays:

The Caged Bird: An episode in the life of Elizabeth Empress of Austria. Performed in 1957.

General:

Barbara Cartland's Book of Useless Information with a Foreword by the Earl Mountbatten of Burma.
(In aid of the United World Colleges)
Love and Lovers (Picture Book)
The Light of Love (Prayer Book)
Barbara Cartland's Scrapbook
(In aid of the Royal Photographic Museum)
Romantic Royal Marriages
Barbara Cartland's Book of Celebrities
Getting Older, Growing Younger

Verse:

Lines on Life and Love

Music:

An Album of Love Songs sung with the Royal Philharmonic Orchestra.

Films:

A Hazard of Hearts
The Lady and the Highwayman
A Ghost in Monte Carlo

Cartoons:

Barbara Cartland Romances (Book of Cartoons) has recently been published in the U.S.A., Great Britain, and other parts of the world.

Children:

A Children's Pop-Up Book: "Princess to the Rescue"

Videos:

A Hazard of Hearts
The Lady and The Highwayman
A Ghost in Monte Carlo

CHAPTER ONE

1818

Lady Drena Winn rode through the trees in the Park and into the drive.

As she turned towards the front door of the house, with her groom following her, she gave a little exclamation.

Outside the front door she could see a very smart carriage drawn by two white horses, and she knew without being told that it was her Grandmother.

The one person Drena loved more than anyone else was the Dowager Countess of Winterton, who had written the previous week to say that she was coming to the country, but was not quite certain on which day she would arrive.

Everything, however, in Winterton House was ready for her.

To Drena it was very exciting that she was actually

here, and she quickened her horse's pace and rode up to the front door at a trot.

She slipped from the saddle and as the Groom caught her horse's reins she ran up the steps. She did not have to ask where her Grandmother was, for she could hear her voice in a room which opened out of the hall, and which was where the family usually sat.

There was no mistaking the soft melodious tones with the undoubted touch of a French accent. The Dowager Countess was French. Her husband, on a visit to Paris, had seen her and fallen overwhelmingly in love, though it was with some difficulty that he finally persuaded the Duc de Saulieu that he was a suitable match for his daughter.

However, after a great deal of argument and an endless exchange of words, the *Comtesse* was finally allowed to follow her heart and marry Edward Winn.

The marriage was completely justified three years later when his elder brother, who was in the Army, was killed in action, and Edward eventually succeeded to the ancient Earldom.

The young *Comtesse* was exceedingly happy with her husband. Whether he was of no importance or an Earl, she gave her love and affection to her English relatives, so that they all adored her. In fact they took to her their troubles and their problems, which in some magical way of her own she invariably solved.

Drena burst into the Drawing-Room and saw her Grandmother looking very attractive, standing reflected in the sunshine coming through the window.

"Grandmama, Grandmama," she cried. "I am so delighted to see you! I did not really expect you until tomorrow."

"How are you, ma petite?" the Dowager Countess asked.

She kissed Drena and then stood back with her hands on her shoulders. "You're looking very lovely," she said. "Even prettier than when I was last here."

"That is what I want you to think, Grandmama." Drena replied. "I have a new gown which I chose for you especially, because you like me in blue."

"I am looking forward to seeing it," the Dowager smiled. "But I have not come here, ma chérie, to talk about your clothes, but about you."

"About me?" Drena asked, flinging her riding-hat down carelessly on a chair.

As her Grandmother sat down on the sofa, she did the same, thinking no one looked more attractive at the age of seventy-three than the Dowager Countess. Her hair was now dead white and it framed her heart-shaped face and accentuated the exquisite texture of her skin.

The Dowager Countess had always been an outstanding beauty, but those who loved her thought sometimes that she was even more beautiful now in old age than she had been as a girl. For there was an expression of compassion in her eyes and an almost hypnotic sympathy in her voice, and anyone who talked to her found it impossible to move away. As they said themselves: "We hang on every word she speaks."

"Why should you want to talk to me about myself, Grandmama?" Drena asked.

"Because I have plans for you for the future," the Dowager replied, "and I only hope you will agree with them."

There was a little pause then Drena said, "I think you are talking about my marriage! Oh, Grandmama, I have no wish to marry anyone. I am so happy here with Papa and the horses, and of course you."

"But you have to marry some time, my dearest," the Dowager said.

"Of course," Drena agreed lightly, "but there is plenty of time. To be honest I find the men I have met at Balls, who come here to shoot or to ride Papa's horses, are on the whole very dull!"

The Dowager Countess held up her hands in horror. "Là! Là!" she exclaimed. "How can you talk like that when you are so young? At your age your heart should be ready to beat faster when any man pays you a compliment."

Drena laughed. "If my heart does not beat as you suggest, that is your fault, Grandmama."

"My fault?" the Dowager enquired.

"Of course it is," Drena explained. "You and Papa have educated me far too well. Not only in the knowledge that comes from books, but in understanding people and knowing what they are like inside!"

She laughed and continued, "I take in what they say perceptively, rather than just listening with my ears."

The Dowager's eyes twinkled. "It is a very great mistake if I have made you a cynic at eighteen."

"I am not a cynic," Drena said seriously, "but I do find most men very egotistical and unappreciative of the things which you and I think are beautiful and exciting."

There was a little pause, and then the Dowager said, "You are talking of Englishmen, ma chérie. Now I am going to talk about a Frenchman."

Drena's eyes opened wide. She always enjoyed it when her Grandmother talked to her about France. Most especially, there was so much to hear about her experiences when she was young, before the Revolution.

Being married to an English husband, she had minded bitterly that because of Napoleon Bonaparte, Britain and France were at War.

"How can the people I love in two countries kill each other in this monstrous way?" the Dowager would ask.

Now the War was over, and the English were beginning to visit France again. The men who had come back from the Army of Occupation had told Drena's Father about the gaieties to be found in Paris.

As Drena listened, she had been quite certain that her Grandmother would soon want to go back to visit her own family. She was therefore not completely astonished when the Dowager Countess said, "I have been thinking, dear child, that you and I should go to France and pay a visit to my relative who is now the Duc de Saulieu."

Drena smiled. "I thought, Grandmama, you would soon want to do that."

"Of course I want to see what has happened to the Château in which I was born and where my family has lived for four hundred years."

She was silent for a moment.

Drena did not speak, knowing that there was more to come.

"I have, in fact," the Dowager said, "had a letter from the present Duc, whose Grandfather was my first cousin, asking me to help him in the restoration of the Château."

"Asking you to help him?" Drena asked. "You mean he wants you to give him money?"

The Dowager Countess looked at her. "Roger tells me," she said, "that he has had a great many expenses since he inherited the Dukedom, and of course a great deal of restoration has to be done after the outrages committed during the Revolution."

"But surely he cannot expect you to pay for what has happened in France?" Drena asked.

The Dowager put her hand over her Grandchild's. "I am, dearest," she said, "a very rich woman. As you remember, my Godfather, who never married, left me an enormous fortune. Because he was English it was fortunately not affected by the Revolution as the money of my family was."

Drena did not say anything, and after a moment her Grandmother went on, "As I have told you before, when your Mother was dying she made me promise I would leave everything I possess to you because your father was only concerned with your brother, Henry, who will inherit his title."

Drena knew this was true.

Her brother, who was five years older than she was and was in the Household Cavalry, was the apple of his Father's eye. Everything at Winterton House revolved around him. The Earl had often said when she was quite young, "You will have to marry money, my darling, because what little money I have must all go to Henry when he inherits."

This instruction however no longer applied when the Dowager Countess came into an immense fortune. She had loved her daughter-in-law, Drena's mother, as deeply as if she were her own daughter, and it had been very easy for her to promise that everything she possessed would go to the child who in many ways resembled herself.

She loved Drena no less dearly. But at the same time it had worried her to think what sort of man she should marry, especially as *he* would in fact have the handling of her money, once she was dead.

Now she had a solution to the problem, and she wanted to put it very tactfully to her granddaughter.

"I thought, my dearest," she said, "that it is possible for you and me to go to France. We will stay at the Château de Saulieu, and you will see all the places that I have talked about ever since you were a small child. You will also meet the Duc."

There was a little silence before Drena said in a low voice, "What you are really suggesting, Grandmama, is that I should marry him."

"I cannot believe," her Grandmother replied, "that Roger is not as handsome, as charming, and as delightful as his Grandfather. If he is all that, what could be more perfect than that you should fall in love and become the *Duchesse* de Saulieu?"

Drena rose from the sofa and walked across the room to the window, where she stood looking out at the garden.

But she was seeing in her mind's eye the Château that her Grandmother had described to her so often. It had a huge moat with water-lilies floating in it and the gardens were brilliant with flowers.

It was something that had been part of her dreams ever since she could remember. Now after so many years of talking about it, thinking about it and dreaming of it, she was actually to see it.

At the same time, she would also see the Duc.

She was well aware, because her Grandmother had told her so, that marriage amongst French aristocrats was always an agreed arrangement between the families.

The Bridegroom had his social position to offer, and it was expected that the Bride should have land or a large dowry that would contribute to the family she was joining.

To a certain extent arranged marriages took place in England also, amongst the nobility. But inevitably there were exceptions to every rule.

Drena knew her Mother had refused a number of advantageous suitors, before she had fallen in love with her Father. They had been exceedingly happy, and her Father's only sadness had been that his wife had been able to give him only two children and no more.

At least he had his son and heir.

Looking out at the sunshine Drena told herself that she did not want to be married just because her fortune would be an advantage to the Duc de Saulieu.

He would consider her amply compensated for the fortune she would bring with her by the privilege of bearing his name.

"What shall . . . I do? What . . . shall I do?"

She asked the question in her heart, for she felt in some way that her Mother would hear and give her the answer.

On the sofa the Dowager Countess neither spoke nor moved. She only waited. But her eyes as she looked at her Granddaughter's back were very revealing.

The rays of the sun were turning Drena's hair to gold, and her slender figure with its tiny waist was silhouetted against the window.

"She is very lovely," the Dowager was thinking. "It would be impossible for any man to resist her."

However she did not speak, but merely waited.

Finally Drena turned round. She walked back to her Grandmother and went down on her knees beside her. "I will go to France with you, Grandmama," she said. "But promise me on everything you hold sacred that you will not force me into marriage."

She drew in her breath before she went on, "If I love the Duc I will gladly marry him. But if I do not love him, then you must swear that you will bring me back here to Papa."

The Dowager Countess smiled. "Of course I promise, ma petite," she said. "But I have a feeling in my bones that you will fall in love with the Duc de Saulieu and that you will be, as I was, very, very happy."

Drena put her arms round her Grandmother and kissed her. "Thank you, Grandmama," she said, "for being so understanding. It will be very exciting to go with you to France. I only hope my French is good enough!"

"Your French is perfect," the Dowager replied. "After all, your Mother spoke French to you as soon as you were born, even though it annoyed your Father."

Drena laughed. "Whenever we talked French Papa always said: 'Stop that foreign chatter! I only enjoy my own language'!"

The Dowager laughed. "I have heard him say that often enough. Yet your Father, when he wants to, can speak very good French. And I taught your Grandfather to speak it as well as I could."

"And he taught you English!" Drena said.

"He taught me about love," her Grandmother said softly, "and that, my dearest, is what I want you to hear and to learn from someone as attractive as our Grandfather was when he was a young man."

Drena knew that she had the Duc de Saulieu in mind. She thought that if she did not fall in love once she reached Burgundy, it was going to be difficult to extricate herself from the situation.

To please her Grandmother she had read the history of the Ducs of Burgundy, and she knew they were very overbearing, very proud, and very demanding.

If the Duc de Saulieu was going to be all of those things, would she be strong enough to insist on returning to England if she wanted to?

Then she told herself that she need not be afraid. Her Grandmother had given her word and that was something she would never break. Aloud she said, "If we are going to France, Grandmama, I shall want more than one new gown. I must do you proud amongst all your smart relations."

"Of course you must," the Dowager Countess agreed. "So I am going to suggest to your father that we go to London tomorrow. We shall have a few days shopping in which I will make you the smartest young woman the French have ever seen. Then we will leave for Burgundy."

"It sounds wonderful," Drena exclaimed, "and it will be delightful to go with you, Grandmama, even though I suspect that Henry will be annoyed at my leaving England just when he has come back from the Army of Occupation."

"Henry has his own interests in London from all I hear," the Dowager Countess said. "He has been fêted by a number of very attractive and beautiful women, and that will soon make him forget the pleasures of Paris."

Drena laughed. She knew her brother, with his French blood, was a very accomplished flirt. Indeed she would have been deaf if she had not heard the rumours of numerous love affairs, which had however never lasted very long.

"Now stop worrying about Henry," her Grandmother said rather sharply, "because we have to concentrate on your Father and persuade him that it is most important that you should come with me to France to meet my relatives, which you have been unable to do before because of the War."

To Drena's surprise it was easier than she had expected. Her Father had merely said that, as far as he himself was concerned, he had no wish to leave his own country. He only hoped that his daughter would not be too disappointed with France, for he believed it had still not recovered from the terrible upheavel caused by the Revolution.

"My relatives write to say that the Churches are opening again," the Dowager Countess argued "and the Châteaux are being repaired."

"I hear there are not enough men left to work in the fields," the Earl replied.

"Well, we will be able to judge for ourselves," the Dowager Countess answered, "and I feel sure the French, who are very sensible people, will recover from their defeat in War more quickly and effectively than other countries would."

Drena could not help thinking that her Father actually was rather envious that she was to have the privilege of seeing France after all these years. At any rate he had not made any objection to her visiting the Château de Saulieu with her Grandmother.

*

As they set out for London the next morning, Drena felt very excited. It was a long drive and they spent two nights on the way. They stayed each time with friends of the Dowager Countess, who had told her she was always welcome.

At one of the houses there was a handsome young man who paid Drena extravagant compliments. He also tried to persuade her to come into the garden to look at the moonlight with him, but she was wise enough not to do that.

At the same time, she could not help wondering to herself what would happen if she had fallen in love with him. Supposing she refused at the last minute to visit France with her Grandmother?

Fortunately they only stayed there for one night. The handsome man pressed her hand when she left, and he made her promise to come and stay with his Mother when she returned home.

There was no chance of his seeing her again before she returned from France, and in London they were too busy to be social.

The Dowager Countess, who had always been noted for her excellent taste, managed to extract a French *chic* from the English couturiers.

She quickly found what she wanted Drena to wear at each shop they visited, and wasted no time looking at gowns and material that were not exactly what they required.

To Drena's surprise she arranged, by paying what seemed enormous sums for each gown, that they should be made in three days. This involved shifts of work-women following one another through each night.

Drena herself had little say in the matter. She only asked rather plaintively "Do I really need so many gowns, Grandmama? We are only staying a week or so, not for years."

"I am sure you will find a use for them, Dearest," her Grandmother replied evasively.

Drena knew from the way she spoke that she was really buying her trousseau, and this sent a feeling of panic through her.

She had a sudden desire to say that she must return home immediately, and would not be able to accompany her Grandmother to France. Then she told herself that that was a foolish fear. No one could compel her to marry anyone.

Once she had made up her mind not to marry the *Duc*, she would insist on coming back at once. That way there would be no embarrassment for her, and also she would not be subjected to any pressure from him.

"If he is determined and obstinate, I can be the same" she told herself. "After all, he is only a man, not a monster who will menace me." She laughed at the idea.

She was thinking of the fairy tales her Grandmother had read her when she was a child. There was inevitably a goblin or a dragon from which the heroine was saved at the last moment by a Knight in Shining Armour. It seemed too much to ask that the Knight in Shining Armour should be the Duc de

Saulieu. There would be no need for anyone to rescue her, if she lost her heart.

Nevertheless when they finally set out on the long journey to Burgundy she felt as if her whole body was split between two conflicting emotions. One was the excitement and thrill at seeing France, but the other was her anxiety, and what had become positively a fear of the Duc.

"I am being foolish! I know I am being stupid!" she told herself, as she looked into the mirror. "Grandmama is determined that he will fall in love with me, and because he is tall and handsome, that I will fall in love with him."

Some cynical part of her mind told her it sounded too easy. Life was never so simple, or was this to be the exception?

They travelled in every possible comfort. The Dowager Countess had her own courier and two outriders to escort and protect them. Plus there was a Lady's Maid who was French, who was even more excited at going back to her native land than the Dowager herself.

They crossed the Channel in a boat in which the Dowager Countess had the only cabin reserved entirely for herself.

When they arrived at Calais there was a travelling carriage drawn by four horses which had been sent by the Duc to convey them in easy stages to Burgundy.

"Some of the Châteaux in which we should have stayed with my old friends," the Dowager Countess said, "are still closed, because all the furniture was removed and sold during the Revolution. The families cannot now afford to replace it, or to repair the Châteaux themselves."

She sighed. "My heart bleeds for them. At the same time we are fortunate in being able to stay in great comfort with other friends who will welcome us very warmly."

This was certainly true. They were not only welcomed with open arms, but dinner parties had been arranged at each of the first two Châteaux they stayed at. There was dancing for the young people to a local Orchestra, and Drena enjoyed every moment of it.

Inevitably she found it sad to have to say goodbye, and start again for the next stage of their journey. "They were such delightful people," she said to her Grandmother, after the second night they had spent with friends. "I wish we could have stayed longer."

"I wish we could too, my Dearest," her Grandmother replied. "At the same time, they are waiting impatiently for us at Saulieu, and we must not linger any longer than is necessary."

Drena knew that her Grandmother was counting so much on the moment when they would arrive at the Château de Saulieu. But she was half afraid that when the moment came she would be disappointed.

She knew of course, because she had been told a thousand times, that it was one of the finest Châteaux in the whole of Burgundy. It had at one time belonged to one of the outstanding Dukes of Burgundy who had made the Province the greatest power in France. But the situation was now quite different.

At the same time, as they entered the Province Drena could understand why it meant so much to her Grandmother.

It was exceedingly beautiful with wide open rolling land, rich and verdant. There were sometimes high mountains in the distance and they crossed deep silver rivers. There were Churches, Castles and Châteaux which took Drena's breath away.

"Burgundy is wonderful!" she had exclaimed as they reached it on the sixth day, during which they passed through dark woods and land that was golden in the sunshine.

"That is what I want you to think, ma petite," the Dowager Countess replied. "It is wonderful for me, and I know it will be wonderful for you."

Drena drew in her breath. How could her Grandmother be so certain that she would be happy, even amongst so much beauty? The country itself was one thing, but the man who would be her husband was something very different. He might be part of the beauty she saw around her, but he might not. Perhaps, she told herself, it was an instinct stronger than thought or feeling. Certainly a perception that was almost spiritual had told her that something lay ahead which would make her afraid.

They had stayed the previous night at a house which they had left with a thousand requests from their hosts to come back as soon as they could. There had been young men for Drena to talk to.

One of them flirted with her in an easy, delightful manner she had not experienced with Englishmen.

Wearing one of her new gowns, she had looked so entrancing that evening that he had more or less proposed to her. "I must see you again," he declared. "I cannot let you leave in this way, when all I shall have are memories!"

"I have to go with Grandmama!" Drena replied. "She is so thrilled and excited at going home. After all these years in exile, to delay her even by a few hours would be cruel!"

"Not half as cruel as it is to me to make me lose you," the Frenchman said.

"You will soon forget me," Drena laughed, "and the next pretty girl who comes along will have you saying the same thing to her."

"That is where you are mistaken!" he insisted. "I think the only way I can see you again will be to follow you to England. When will you be going back?"

Drena made a helpless little gesture with her hands. "I have no idea," she answered.

He stiffened. "You are not suggesting – you cannot be saying – that you might stay in France!"

There was something in the way he spoke which made her look at him curiously. "Why do you say that?" she asked.

For a moment she thought he was not going to answer her. Then he said, "Perhaps I have been very dense," he said, "but now, like a jigsaw puzzle, the pieces are beginning to fall into place."

"What do you mean?" Drena enquired.

He looked away from her. Then he said, "Is it

possible? Can the reason behind this visit be that you are thinking of marrying the Duc de Saulieu?"

Drena did not reply, but he saw the colour come into her cheeks and he said, "I never thought of it! It never occurred to me! It is impossible! Absolutely impossible!"

Drena looked at him as he went on, "I know Roger de Saulieu, and I assure you he is not for you. Do you understand me? You are not to marry him, however persuasively he begs you to do so!"

"Why should you imagine he will beg me to marry him?" Drena asked, trying to speak lightly.

The man she was talking to put his hand up to his forehead. "I have been very dense," he said, "but now I can see it all. I was told you are an heiress, and that your Grandmother is a very rich woman. Of course, that is why you are being taken like a lamb to the slaughter!"

"I can assure you," Drena said coldly, "I do not intend to do anything I do not wish to do. I have not yet found anyone I want to marry."

"Then marry me!" the Frenchman said. "I, at least, can make you happy. A great deal happier than you would ever be with the Duc."

"You are supposing a great many things that have no foundation," Drena said. "I have not yet even met the Duc. I have only heard about him from my Grandmother, who wants to show me the house where she was born and brought up as one of the Saulieu family. There are, I believe, a great number of them."

"That is true," the Frenchman replied, "But there is only one Duc, and he is not for you!"

Unexpectedly he put his hands on her shoulders and turned her round to face him. "Listen to me," he said. "Listen, because it concerns you vitally. You must not, on any account, marry the Duc de Saulieu. Is that clear?"

"Very clear," Drena said. "At the same time I would be interested to know why you dislike the Duc so vehemently and what he has done to upset you."

The Frenchman released her. "He has upset a great number of people," he said. "And I will not throw anything so young, so innocent, and so lovely as you to the lions!"

"And that is how you think of the Duc de Saulieu?" Drena demanded.

"I could think of many other ways to describe him," the Frenchman replied, "but I will leave you to find out for yourself. All I will say quite simply is 'Be careful! Be very, very careful!'"

"I am not quite certain what I have to be careful of!" Drena said. "However it is wise to be forearmed. So, Monsieur, I will take your advice and be careful."

The Frenchman took her hand and put it to his lips. "I shall be waiting for you here on your return," he said. "And please, if you value yourself as much as I value you, let it be soon!"

He kissed her hand again. Then, as a young man claimed Drena for a dance, there was no chance of any further conversation.

When they left the Château the following morning, the Frenchman, as she said goodbye, murmured very quietly, almost beneath his breath, "Beware of the lions!"

As they set off with a new team of horses, Drena knew that her Grandmother was counting the hours, if not the minutes, until they arrived at the Château.

"I see you were a great success with the Comte last night," she said to Drena. "But, although he is a nice young man, he is not of any particular importance and in no way compares with the Duc."

Drena wondered if she should tell her Grandmother what the Comte had said about the Duc. Then she thought it would be unkind. After all, perhaps he was just jealous of the Duc, and that would account for his rather strange attitude.

They had luncheon at a small wayside Inn where the food was surprisingly good. They were made as comfortable as it was possible to be by the proprietor and his wife, and afterwards they set off on the last lap of their journey.

Now the Dowager Countess was beginning to point out special places she remembered. A church on top of a hill, a small fortified town which was part of the history of Burgundy, a Convent situated in a very desolate part of the country. Finally there was Saulieu itself.

At first glance the Château was even more magnificent and more impressive than Drena had expected.

As they drove up towards it, it seemed enormous. On each side of the immense building there were domed, circular towers, with a heraldic device on top of them.

Drena was prepared for the large moat. Her Grandmother had told her it was filled with water-lilies which were just coming into bloom. Among them sailing serenely over the still water were white swans, seemingly part of the huge Château.

They passed through an archway into the great Courtyard round which the Château was built in a complete square. Drena thought it was the most impressive place she had ever seen. Then, as they drew up in front of the main door, her Grandmother's relations came running out excitedly to greet them.

"You have arrived! You have arrived, *Aimée*!" they cried.

There seemed to be dozens of them kissing the Dowager, while Drena tried frantically to remember their names. There were young, old, and middle-aged, and she gathered they had all come to the Château specially to greet her Grandmother.

They went inside. Although the rooms were lofty and impressive and exquisitely designed, Drena could see why her Grandmother had warned her about the devastation suffered during the Revolution, and still not repaired while Napoleon was fighting to conquer all Europe.

She soon realised, as they went from room to room, that while some were furnished, some had nothing remaining of their former glory. In others there would be just an exquisitely painted ceiling or an outstandingly humble fireplace. There were just a few left of what had once been fine chandeliers, and an Aubusson carpet here and there.

But the sofas, chairs and tables did not seem to suit the rooms as they must have when they were originally furnished. The fireplaces seemed somehow out of proportion, and there was an unmistakable scarcity of ornaments. There were few carved gilded tables which were correct for the period.

Yet what there was was so fine that Drena ran out of adjectives with which to say how impressed she was. One thing she had not yet seen was the Duc himself.

There were young men, and quite a number of them, and her Grandmother stared at them in astonishment. Some had only just been born when she was last in France, whilst others had arrived in the world when she was no longer able to visit her own country.

There was a glass of wine for them to drink after their journey, and a number of delicious patisseries to tempt the appetite.

They sat in an enormous room with high windows overlooking the moat and the garden beyond it, and they talked of people of whom Drena had never heard. They chattered so quickly that she was half afraid she would not understand what they were saying.

Then, after a little time had passed, the Dowager Countess suggested that they should go to their rooms. "You must give me time to rest a little before dinner," she said. "I am feeling quite dizzy with the excitement of being back and seeing you all again."

"We love seeing you!" everyone exclaimed.

They all rose to their feet and were just about to leave the room when the door opened.

There was a sudden silence, and the voices that had been chatting so gaily seemed to tail away.

Drena knew unmistakenly that this was the moment. This was when she was going to see the Duc for the first time.

A man came in, but he was not alone. There was a woman with him, but he advanced in front of her towards the company. He was tall, broad-shouldered, with a square forehead and dark hair.

"He is undoubtedly good-looking," Drena thought. But somehow he did not look as she had expected him to look, though he resembled many of the portraits she had already seen on the walls, as they had walked through the different rooms.

He came towards them and his eyes found the Dowager Countess immediately. He took her hand, raised it to his lips.

"Welcome home, my dear Cousin," he said. "It is delightful to see you. I have been waiting impatiently for your arrival."

"And I have been waiting impatiently to see you," the Dowager Countess said. "You have grown quite a lot in the years between."

She was laughing and the Duc laughed too. "I think I must have been only two or three at the time," he said. "But I remember, of course, how very beautiful you were."

It was, Drena thought, a polite, if insincere speech.

Her Grandmother was obviously delighted. "Thank

you, Roger," she said. "And now I must introduce you to my most beloved Granddaughter who has accompanied me. Drena, this is Roger, the Duc of Saulieu, and I hope, because I love you both, you will become very close . . . friends."

She was, Drena thought, going too fast.

At the same time she dropped a curtsey to the Duc as he took her hand.

"You must have known," he said in a deep voice, "that I was also waiting to see you."

Drena's hand was in his. As he spoke his fingers closed as if he wanted her to be aware of his strength.

Then she looked up into his eyes.

She knew, for no reason she could explain, that something was wrong, very, very wrong. But what it was she could not imagine.

CHAPTER TWO

There was no doubt, Drena thought, that the Duc was doing everything in his power to make himself agreeable. At dinner he talked animatedly and very flatteringly to her Grandmother. He was obviously excited at the idea of taking them round the Château to-morrow.

"There are many things for you to see," he said, "and of course you will remember how it was before the Revolutionaries vandalised everything we prized."

He smiled as he went on, "I expect you remember that the reigning Duke, who was my cousin, had a great number of things put away in secret places where even the most painstaking Revolutionary could not find them."

"That was fortunate," the Dowager Countess said. "But they must have done a terrible amount of damage."

"The worst thing was that they guillotined my cousin, Duc Francois," the Duc said. "I was only three at the time and my Father and Mother were in hiding. Of course, I remember nothing about it directly."

"It must have been terrible for the whole family," Drena said in a sympathetic voice.

She was thinking that now she was in France she could realise more clearly than she had been able to before what they had suffered. It must have been an unexpressable horror for all the Aristocrats to know that at any moment they might lose their lives.

She had heard a great deal about it from her Grandmother, and it had always distressed her.

Now she could see the deliberate damage done in many of the rooms. She could now hear the older members of the Saulieu family talking of their experiences, and it seemed to her that it had only happened yesterday.

"You, of course, were not born," the Duc said to her unexpectedly.

Because she was deep in her thoughts she started. "That is true," she agreed. "The 'Terror' was all over by the time I came into the world."

"Making it even more beautiful than it was already," the Duc said flatteringly.

She felt a little shy, but she did not blush. She knew, almost as if someone was telling her, that he was not really as interested in her beauty as he pretended to be.

When they were having a glass of champagne before

dinner she had been aware that there was an intimate relationship between him and the lady with whom he had arrived into the Salon. Because she had naturally concentrated on the Duc himself, Drena had not really paid any attention to the lady in question, who was introduced as the Comtesse de Pastel.

Now when she looked at her more closely, Drena had realised she was very attractive in a typically French manner. She was not beautiful, but her dark hair and her eyes flecked with green were very compelling. Almost everything she said sounded witty, and she moved with a sinuous grace, and was dressed in a gown which was unmistakably French. It was fashioned in a way which seemed to reveal her personality as well as her figure.

As she moved amongst the family, Drena had the idea that the Comtesse was not particularly welcome. But perhaps she was only imagining it, for the Comtesse made the Duc laugh before dinner when he was drinking a glass of wine. But when she touched his arm with her long, thin fingers, Drena thought there was something sensuous about it.

Then she told herself that she must be making a story out of nothing.

The Comtesse wore a gold ring besides an enormous emerald on the third finger of her left hand. "She is just a friend," Drena told herself, "and of course the Duc, being French, flirts with every woman, whether she is as old as Grandmama or as young as I am."

He certainly went out of his way to be a charming

and attentive host, and when dinner was finished he took the Dowager Countess and Drena to see the Library. "You will appreciate, Cousin Aimée," he said, "that this is the one room which was left more or less intact during the Revolution."

There was a twist to his lips as he added, "No one wanted to read books, when they were so busy destroying the treasures of France which had built up the history of our country."

Drena loved books. She was thrilled by the walls that were packed from floor to ceiling with beautifully bound and colourful volumes. There was also a balcony along one wall of the Library which could be reached by a spiral staircase made of polished brass.

"It is exactly as I remember it," the Dowager Countess said, with a little catch in her voice. "I can see your cousin, Duc François, sitting in the chair in front of the fire and reading me some exploit of our ancestors that he had found in an ancient history book."

"His portrait has been restored and, as you see, is over the mantelpiece," the Duc said. "We found it thrown away in one of the out-houses. Whoever had taken it originally from the Library must have thought it would not fetch them any money in the market-place."

"That was indeed fortunate," the Dowager Countess said.

She moved to stand in front of the mantelpiece and Drena followed her. The portrait was of a very handsome man, and Drena thought that he had an unforgettable face. It might have been a portrait of what every woman imagined as the ideal of an aristocrat, for he was painted wearing his decorations, and there was one hanging round his neck beneath his high cravat.

As she stood looking at the portrait, she wished she had known that Duc of Saulieu. Then as she glanced at the present Duc, she recognised a family likeness but with something missing. She could see it in the expression in his eyes, and the line of his mouth, yet she could not explain it exactly to herself, though the difference was there. A difference which she knew, although she could not put it into words, was very important.

"And now I have other rooms to show you," the Duc said, as if he thought that they had stared long enough at the portrait of Duc François.

He moved towards the door and as Drena followed her Grandmother she said, "I hope, Monsieur le Duc, you will allow me to borrow books from this wonderful Library while I am at the Château. I would like to read them all! As that is impossible, I will be contented with one or two."

The Duc smiled and made a gesture with his hands. "Everything I have is yours," he said. "And of course I hope, Mademoiselle, that you will in fact stay long enough to read them all."

Drena realised it was her own fault to have given him the opening to make such a remark. At the same time she felt frightened, as if the walls were closing in on her and she was being trapped. "I shall be quite content with three at the most," she replied politely.

Nevertheless she realised that her Grandmother was delighted at what the Duc had said. She was looking first at her and then at the Duc, as if she was already certain that her plan for their marriage had succeeded.

Quickly Drena, realising she had made a mistake, talked about the pictures in the passage outside the Library.

The Duc hurried them on to the Music Room. "I have been told, Cousin Aimée," he said, "that you often played the spinnet here when you were a girl. I hope it is something you will do again, although we now have a pianoforte to replace the spinnet which I believe was chopped up for firewood."

"That was sacrilege!" the Dowager Countess exclaimed in dismay. "I remember it well. It was beautifully inlaid with ivory and had been made by one of the Masters of Music in Vienna."

The Music Room was very beautiful with a pianoforte standing on a small platform. Drena wanted to ask her Grandmother to sit down to play, but the Duc hurried them on to see the Chapel.

"I have already had this restored," he said, "and I know you will be pleased to learn that I have appointed quite recently a Priest to be my Private Chaplain."

"That is something I am delighted to hear, my dear boy," the Dowager Countess said.

The Chapel had been originally constructed at the same time as the Château. Unfortunately the Altar had been stolen and the carved seats in the Chancel burnt.

"We were lucky the devastation was not worse," the Duc was saying. "The Church in the village was destroyed almost completely, and they set fire to the house in which the Priest lived."

The Dowager Countess gave an exclamation of horror but the Duc went on: "He only saved his life by hiding in the woods until the Revolutionaries had passed on to do their devastation elsewhere."

"I still cannot believe all this happened in my beloved France," the Dowager Countess said in a low voice.

"We were luckier than many," the Duc said. "They might have burnt down the Château. Instead they only took most of our furniture and no one was actually murdered in Saulieu itself."

The Dowager Countess looked at him in surprise. "But what about your Cousin, Duc François?"

"He was not here when it happened," the Duc replied. "He was away from home at one of our other houses. They searched for him here, and then told their fellow Revolutionaries to look for him elsewhere."

"And they found him," the Dowager Countess said sadly.

"They found him," the Duc agreed, "and that meant that when the Revolution was over my Father came out of hiding and took over the Château."

There was a little pause before the Dowager Countess said, "I am sure we are all very grateful that the Château itself is still here and is still as beautiful as I remember it."

"That is what I keep saying to myself," the Duc

said. "At the same time I cannot afford to keep it up, let alone restore it. As you see there is much restoration needed in most of the rooms, and it is still possible, if one searches in the dealers' shops, to find some of our original furniture."

The Dowager Countess was interested. "Is that really true?"

"I saw a commode in Paris only last week," the Duc said, "which I was told had stood here in the Salon d'Or. But the price they were asking for it was one I could not possibly afford."

The Dowager Countess did not answer. But Drena knew he was implicitly asking her Grandmother to buy it back for the Château.

Then as she saw the Duc look at her she felt herself shiver. She knew that in his mind and in her Grandmother's there was one very simple answer to the problem. It would give him control of her huge fortune when her Grandmother died, and doubtless a large proportion of it as soon as they married.

Because she was frightened, she moved quickly towards another door which led into the garden. The stars were coming out, and a young moon was moving up in the sky casting a light on the fountains playing in the centre of the green lawns. They were throwing their water high above the carved stone bases so that it glittered in the air like tiny rainbows.

"It is beautiful! Very beautiful!" Drena thought to herself. "But I would be marrying not only the Château, but the man who owns it." Almost as if a cold wind passed through her she shivered.

She heard the Duc taking her Grandmother away to look at some other room. He was saying it also needed furniture which he could not afford to buy. Instead of following them Drena stepped out into the garden, because she felt as if she needed to breathe the fresh air. She wanted the stars to tell her not to be so afraid as she was at the moment. She looked up at them, sending without really being aware of it, a prayer for help. "I am frightened," she said in her heart. "Frightened of what will happen to me." She knew that everything was moving very quickly.

Far more quickly than she had expected. She was quite sure that not only her Grandmother but also the Duc was determined they should be married as soon as possible, and she had a sudden impulse to run away; to disappear into the darkness and not go back into the Château.

Then she told herself she was being absurd. She was in a strange country of which she had no knowledge. She might get lost even in the garden if she did not keep within sight of the Château and its lighted windows. "I have to go back. I must go back!" she told herself severely.

At the same time she knew it was an effort. For some reason she did not want to put into words, she was really afraid.

By the time she had returned the Duc and her Grandmother were back in the Salon with the rest of the family. They were all talking and laughing.

As she entered Drena told herself she was being hysterical and extremely foolish. Why should she be frightened of the Duc or anyone else? Her Grandmother had given her her word, which she knew she would not break. If she did not wish to marry, she would not be pressed into doing so.

It was soon after they had returned to the Salon that the Dowager Countess said she was tired and wished to retire. "I will come with you, Grandmama," Drena said quickly.

"Oh, stay with us," the Duc said pleadingly. "There are so many other things I want to talk to you about."

"I am afraid they will have to wait until tomorrow," Drena replied. "Like Grandmama I am very tired, and I find driving even behind such magnificent horses as Your Grace's rather exhausting."

"Then I will permit you to leave us for tonight," the Duc said. "At the same time the light will go with you."

As he spoke in a somewhat caressing tone, Drena suddenly noticed that the Comtesse de Pastel was listening. She was sitting in a low chair and looking up at the Duc, but the expression on her face told Drena all too clearly that she was furious at the way he was speaking.

"She is jealous," Drena told herself. She knew that beyond doubt the Comtesse and the Duc were very intimate. Hurriedly she said goodnight to most of the other relations, and followed her Grandmother to the door.

The Duc took them to the foot of the staircase. "This has been a memorable evening because you are with us," he said to the Dowager Countess. "Never again, Cousin Aimée, must you leave us for so long. I know now that you are part of my family and my home, and we cannot live without you."

He spoke dramatically and the Dowager Countess was delighted. "Thank you, dear boy," she said. "And you know I want to help you in all your difficulties."

As she finished speaking she started to climb the stairs and Drena joined her. She moved so quickly that she did not have to give the Duc her hand.

Instead over her shoulder, as they moved up the stairs, she said, "Good night, Monsieur."

She was, however, aware that the Duc stood watching them until they reached the landing and were out of sight.

As they walked slowly towards her bedroom the Dowager Countess said, "Roger is charming. Even more charming than I expected him to be. I am sure, my dearest, you feel the same?"

"He is certainly very flattering in what he says," Drena said sharply.

"I am sure he means every word," the Dowager Countess answered. "How could he not be bowled over, dearest child, by your beauty?"

She gave a little sigh of satisfaction and added, "I thought at dinner that amongst all those dark-haired women you looked like a star that had fallen down from the Heavens."

Drena slipped her arm through her Grandmother's. "That is a lovely thing to say, Grandmama, and when

I looked up at the stars just now I felt sure they were protecting me."

"Of course they are," the Dowager Countess replied, "but you have no need of protection. Everything in your life is assured."

She gave a sigh. "The horrors are over, and the sooner we forget what the Revolution did to those we love, the better."

Drena knew that she had been very moved by what she had seen and what she had heard since she arrived at the Château. "As you say, Grandmama," she said aloud, "it is all over now. What we must think about it the future."

"That is just what I am doing, my precious child," her Grandmother replied. "I am thinking of you and how much I want you here as the Duchesse de Saulieu."

Drena gave a little cry. "You are going too fast, Grandmama!" she protested. "Much, much too fast! I want to think of being here just today, tomorrow, and not plan for the future until it is time to leave."

There was a little pause and then as they reached the Dowager Countess's bedroom she said very quietly, "Perhaps there will be no reason to leave."

The Dowager Countess's maid was waiting inside the room to put her to bed.

Drena forced back the protest that came to her lips, but instead she kissed her Grandmother and went to her own bedroom. Only then did she ask furiously how it was possible for the Dowager Countess to want her to be married here in the Château.

If she was married, it *must* be in her own home and in the Church where she had been christened.

She told herself it was forcing her to arrange their immediate marriage and thus provide him with money. He must be in very dire straits, Drena told herself.

As the maid they had brought with them was that of the Dowager Countess, she rang the bell for someone to help her undress. The maid who answered it was a middle-aged woman who had come to the Château as soon as it had been re-opened.

"You should've seen the mess it were in when we arrived, M'mselle," she said. "It took us weeks, no months to get the dirt off the floors, to clean the windows, and burn the rubbish."

She shook her head and then continued "And Monsieur le Duc were always pressing us to do more and to do it quickly."

"Why was there so much hurry?" Drena asked.

"I s'pose he was frightened like we all were, that war'd break out again, and there would be more men taken away to be killed. I tells you, M'mselle, there's not a house in the village that has not lost one of its loved ones."

"It must have been terrible for you," Drena said.

"Half-starved we were," the maid went on, as she hung up Drena's gown in the wardrobe. "If we hadn't been able to grow a few things in the cottage gardens, we'd've died, and that's a fact!"

"I am so sorry for you," Drena said. "But now it is all over, you can be happy and comfortable again."

"Not as comfortable as all that!" the maid said.

"We've only a quarter of the staff there were in the old days, and Monsieur Le Duc can't afford to pay any more. So as I says to myself when I gets up in the morning, I've to do the work of three people rather than one."

She was obviously a grumbler. But Drena thought there was doubtless some truth in what she said. In fact she had thought at dinner they were rather short of footmen, especially when she thought of the number that her Father had waiting at home when there was a party.

Alone in the comfortable bed and in darkness, she tried to think sensibly, without being agitated about the position in which she found herself. She knew already that she had no wish to marry the Duc.

She could not explain why, she just knew it was something she could not do, She was also aware that it was going to be difficult for her to refuse him when he proposed to her. Worse still, it would be more difficult to convince her Grandmother.

She knew when she confirmed the marriage her Grandmother would give money to restore the Château and provide the Duc with the money he needed so badly. "All he wants is money," she told herself.

She saw again the face of the Comtesse de Pastel and the expression in her eyes as she looked at the Duc. It was one of anger, of jealousy and Drena thought, some other emotion which she could not define.

"I suppose," she told herself, "that if the Comtesse were free and also rich, he would marry her!"

She remembered hearing her Father say once that the French were very practical, and that they never gave anything without expecting something in return. If the Duc gave his title to a woman, then she would have to pay for it in one way or another.

"He can have the money, as far as I am concerned," Drena told herself. "But he cannot have me!"

That seemed a brave decision, but she knew it was going to be a very difficult one to carry out. She was in fact very tired, and she fell fast asleep immediately. She did not even dream, as she expected to do, of the Château, the Duc or their journey from England.

But when she woke the sun was shining, and it seemed stupid to worry about anything. She could see the beauty of the garden from her window and there would be horses for her to ride. Although it was still early, she got up and put on one of the attractive riding-habits the Dowager Countess had brought her in London.

"Busvine," she had said, "is the best tailor to all the smartest ladies of the *Beau Monde*, and in that particular you will not, my dearest, be beaten by the French!"

Drena had laughed. Yet she knew as she walked downstairs that her Grandmother was right. She was wearing a deep blue habit of some thin material because it was summer, and it was ornamented with white braid, with a white gauze veil to match round the crown of her blue felt hat.

She had expected, because they had talked about it before dinner, that some of the younger members of the family would be riding, but when she reached the Hall, it was only the Duc who was waiting there.

"I was told you were getting ready to ride," he said. "So I have ordered you a horse which is waiting for you outside."

"How kind of you," Drena replied, even though she thought what he said was annoying. Why should whatever she did be reported to her host before she could speak of it herself?

There was no sign of any of the others, so she and the Duc walked down the long steps to the front door. Outside there were two exceedingly fine horses held by two grooms.

Drena patted them both, saying politely as she did so, "I knew you would have magnificent horses to equal the magnificence of your Château."

"I brought these only a week ago, when I learnt that you were coming from England," the Duc replied. "Your Grandmother had told me how much you appreciated fine horseflesh and I did not wish you, of all people, to be disappointed."

Drena could not help thinking that he had doubtless not paid for them. Instead he was hoping to be able to do so, if his plan succeeded. Then she told herself she was being unnecessarily unkind.

She smiled at the Duc as he helped lift her on to the saddle, and then arranged, with an experienced hand, her skirt over the stirrup. Then he mounted himself and they rode away from the Château into the Park, where there were spotted deer moving about under the trees.

They rode without speaking until they came on to some level ground. Then, without saying anything, Drena gave her horse its head. She galloped beside the Duc until it became a race. Faster and faster they urged their horses on.

It was only when the field came to an end, that Drena realised she must draw her mount in. She was, however, aware that she was just a fraction ahead of the Duc, and she told herself with satisfaction that it was an omen that he would not get his own way.

As their horses came almost to a standstill the Duc said, "You ride exactly as I was told you would. I can only commend you as the most outstanding horsewoman I have ever seen."

"It is easy to be good, when one is on a horse as fine as this," Drena said. "It must have been very hard for their previous owner to part with them."

"He did so because he needed the money," the Duc said dryly. "And how could I resist buying something which I knew would please you?"

Drena did not answer, and after a moment he said, "You are far more beautiful than your Grandmother told me you were, and I can only say that I have been dazzled, bewildered and stunned by your loveliness from the first moment I saw you."

Drena moved her horse a little away from him. But he followed her and came nearer still. "There is so much I want to give you, Drena," he said. "So much that we can do together."

Drena put up her hands. "Please," she said, "we have only just met. I have only been at the Château for a few hours. Let us enjoy our ride, which is why we are here."

"I hope that you are here for a very different reason," the Duc answered. "When your Grandmother told me she was bringing you with her, I knew what was in her mind."

"She wanted me to see the Château she had told me so much about, and to meet the members of her family whom she herself had not seen for a number of years."

"She also wanted you to meet me," the Duc said. "Just as, my beautiful one, I wanted to meet you!"

Drena touched her horse with her whip so that it sprang forward. "I want to ride," she said, "not talk."

She rode away from the Duc, but he followed her quickly. Once again they were racing side by side, and the way he kept glancing at her told her that he had every intention of renewing the conversation as soon as they slowed up. She thought despairingly that it had been a mistake to come out alone with him, but she knew now that he must have diverted the rest of the party in another direction. Or had even told them not to come riding.

He wanted her to himself and that was what he had got. She knew it would be a mistake to get involved in a discussion or an argument about it, or to precipitate a reply to his question. If he would only let things take their course, she would be able to think more clearly.

Perhaps, although it seemed unlikely, she would be

able to leave without there being any unpleasantness about it. As the horses slowed down again, she said, "I want to see more of the Estate. I can see how attractive it is, so show me where the boundaries are."

The Duc laughed. "You cannot see them from here. I own something like ten thousand acres."

"As much as that!" Drena exclaimed. "Then you are very lucky."

"I would be if I could afford to enjoy it," the Duc said. "The land has been sadly neglected during the War, and it needs more workmen than I can afford."

He paused then continued, "If we are to grow the grapes which provide the wine for which we were once famous, we need new vines and experts to advise me."

It all gets back to money, Drena thought. She still rode on, saying almost over her shoulder, "Do show me a vineyard. I have never seen one."

They reached the nearest vineyard moving quickly without any intimate conversation. But Drena knew only too well by the way the Duc was looking at her what he was thinking. She was trying desperately to prevent him from putting the actual question to which she must give her answer.

She was relieved to find there were men working in the Vineyard and she talked to them. They explained to her how they were watching over the young shoots, always fearful that one of the uncontrollable diseases might attack them and destroy the whole crop.

Then they rode on, and soon they were in a small

hamlet. Drena could see without being told that the roofs of the cottages needed repair, and there were also many windows with cracked panes or no glass at all.

"You can see what needs to be done here," the Duc said.

One or two of the peasant people stared as they went by, but to Drena's surprise the women did not curtsey to the Duc. They only looked at him, she thought, with a surly expression that was almost insulting.

Her Grandmother had told her how before the Revolution the peasants on the Saulieu Estate were well-fed, rose-cheeked and happy. The Duchesses of the time had frequently visited them. When Drena's Grandmother had accompanied her Mother, she had always gone back to the Château feeling happy that so many people were content.

"They felt," she said, "they were part of the Saulieu family."

There was nothing like that now.

As they passed one of the cottages at the end of the hamlet, a woman standing in the garden shouting something rude at the Duc. Then she went into the house and slammed the door.

Drena was so surprised that she looked at the Duc for an explanation. She did not have to put it into words.

"These people want money," he said. "That is something I cannot give them."

Drena signed. She thought as they rode on that she

was being put into a position where she would have to refuse not just one man. She would also refuse a great many other people who depended upon him.

"What can ... I do? What ... can I do?" she asked herself.

Now they were riding back towards the Château. When it was finally in sight the Duc drew in his horse. "I want you to look at the Château from here," he said. "It undoubtedly is the most important and the most beautiful in the whole of Burgundy."

He paused for Drena to take in the view, and then continued, "It has always been part of our history, and that is what it must become again in the future. But as you well know, it has been crippled for nearly thirty years. First by the Revolution and then by the War."

He stopped, and then said very quietly, "Surely you can understand, Drena, how much it needs your help."

Drena drew in her breath. This was an approach she had not expected. Then because she knew the Duc was waiting she forced herself to say, "I understand! I understand exactly, Monsieur, what you feel about these people who are yours. But you must give me time!"

"Time?" the Duc asked sharply. "Why? Surely you realise what I have to offer you. I cannot believe that any man, wherever you met him, could offer you more."

"It is not exactly a question of what I am offered," Drena said.

"Then let me put it a little differently," the Duc said. "I want you. I want you as my wife. It is needless for me to say that I fell in love with you, madly and completely, from the moment I saw you."

It sounded very sincere and very positive, but some part of Drena's brain was asking what he would have said to her if he had not known that she would bring him as his wife a great fortune.

Looking at the Château glittering like a great jewel in the sunshine she could see the fountains throwing their water up to the sky. On the moat the water was shining as the white swans swam through it. Of course he thought, Drena told herself, that any woman would be overwhelmed by anything so beautiful, so magnificent.

And by the fact that at the same time she could become a Duchess.

But how could she explain to him? How could she make him understand that she wanted more than that? She wanted something which she could explain quite easily in one word. She wanted "love".

A love which would unite not their eyes, but their hearts. A love that in itself had nothing to do with money and possessions, or titles.

It was, in fact, something not material but spiritual and a gift from God.

CHAPTER THREE

Drena awoke early but thought it would be a mistake to go riding again alone with the Duc. She had the feeling that he would be waiting for her as he had yesterday morning, and would inevitably continue to press his advances upon her.

"I must have time to think." she told herself. But she knew that something within her shrank from being in close contact with him.

She therefore dressed in an ordinary gown rather than her riding-habit and went down a side-staircase. She thought she would go first to the Library and borrow some of the fascinating books she had seen yesterday. She opened the Library door.

To her surprise there was an old man with white hair sitting at the desk in the window. He rose when he saw her and bowing said, "Bonjour, Mademoiselle. In case you are wondering who I am, I am the Curator of the Château."

Drena held out her hand. "I am delighted to meet you, Monsieur. I have been fascinated by so many things I have seen already, and I am sure you can give me some more information about them."

"I will certainly do my best," the Curator replied. "It may interest you to know that I was here before the Revolution – of course as a young man – and now I spend my remaining years in trying to restore as much as possible as it was originally."

"I am afraid that must be a very difficult task," Drena said.

"It is indeed," the Curator agreed.

"I really came," Drena said, "to ask if I could borrow some of these fascinating books. In particular will you recommend one which tells of the family history?"

"*Certainement*," the Curator smiled. "In fact I am writing one myself in order to bring the story up to date."

"Are you really?" Drena exclaimed. "How exciting! I suppose you will include an account of the furniture and the pictures that are missing as well as what is still here."

The old man shook his head. "It makes me want to weep," he said, "when I think of how much has gone and is forever unobtainable."

Drena was remembering what the Duc had told her Grandmother yesterday and she said, "Monsieur le Duc was saying last night that he had seen an inlaid commode of great value in Paris, but that it was too expensive for him to purchase."

The Curator frowned. "I am afraid, Mademoiselle, you have been misinformed," he said. "The piece to which you are referring I have seen for myself. It was offered to Monsieur le Duc by a crook who thought to pass it off as the genuine article."

Drena looked surprised. "Are you sure we are talking about the same piece?"

"Quite sure," the Curator replied. "It is the only time that Monsieur le Duc has shown an interest in anything appertaining to the furnishings of the Château. But, as I have said, the chest in question is undoubtedly a fake."

Drena was still for a moment. Then thinking of how the Duc had behaved when he showed them round the Château she said, "I thought that Monsieur le Duc was anxious to make the Château look again as it was before the Revolution."

The Curator sighed. "How I wish that were true!" he said. "Some of the older members of the family are naturally anxious to see it back in all its glory, but Monsieur le Duc prefers Paris and the joys which that attractive city provides for a young man." He spoke despondently.

Drena longed to ask him more questions, but thought it would be bad manners to gossip about her host. Instead she said, "I see you have a very attractive miniature on your desk. May I look at it?"

"But of course, Mademoiselle. It was fortunately hidden away in one of the secret places in the Château, and it was not found by the greedy hordes which carried off so much from us."

There was a pain in his voice that was very obvious. Drena thought it touching that he should care so much about the Château, so he picked up the miniature and saw that it had been painted at the beginning of the 17th century depicting one of the Duchesses of Saulieu.

"It is lovely!" she exclaimed.

"You will see her name on the back," the Curator said. "What I am doing, Mademoiselle, for those who come after me, is to put the names of the Saulieu ancestors on the backs of the portraits and miniatures, with of course the dates of their lifetime."

"I think that is very sensible," Drena smiled, "for it would be difficult, if you were not here, for any new members of the family to know who is who."

"Precisely!" the Curator smiled. "And I am hoping that some of the portraits will be reproduced in my book."

"I only wish it was finished so that I could read it," Drena said. "I am sure you have some marvellous stories to tell of the Saulieu family."

The Curator nodded. "They go back a long way in history, and while there have been some fine and splendid men among them who have helped to govern France, and others have been heroes who have fought and died for her, there have also been eccentrics."

"It would be interesting to read about them," Drena remarked.

"There was one," the Curator said, "and I will show you a portrait of him, who was determined to be treated as if he was a King, and had the Château arranged as if it was a Royal Palace. His courtiers were not allowed to sit in his presence, and his servants had to approach him on their knees!"

Drena laughed. "I am sure that makes a very amusing story to read."

"There was another," the old man went on, "who had a passion to know everything that was going on, however trivial. He made small holes in the walls so that he could listen to what was being said in the next room, and concealed them with panelling or material. Even to this day I have been unable to discover the whereabouts of a great number of them."

"But you know they are there," Drena said.

"The Duc of the time jotted down in a Diary the conversations he overheard, some of which were very trivial — others critical of him. I often wonder if he took his revenge on some without their knowing the reason why."

"I can see, Monsieur, that your book will be an instantaneous success as soon as it is published."

"What I hope," the Curator said in a deep voice, "is that it will be a guide and a help for posterity, and especially for the Saulieus who will continue to live here, generation after generation."

He spoke in a rapt voice as if it was something which meant a great deal to him. As she realised how old he was, Drena could not help wondering if his book would ever be finished.

"Do show me the books already in the Library which recount the family history," she begged.

The Curator moved towards a bookcase beside

the mantelpiece. "I have three here," he said. "I am afraid you will find them heavy reading, but they are certainly interesting."

"Then I would love to have two to start with," Drena said, "and I will return for the third when I have finished them."

The Curator smiled at her. "I think perhaps, Mademoiselle," he said, "you are looking for information which will be of use to you personally."

Drena stiffened. Then she said, "I do not know why you should think that, Monsieur."

"Forgive me, forgive me," the Curator said quickly. "It is just that in a place like this everybody gossips, and it was thought, even before you arrived, that there was a special reason for your coming with the Dowager Countess."

Drena was well aware of what he was implying, and she resented it. Nevertheless it made her more afraid than she was already. If the servants in the household had already accepted her as the future wife of the present Duc, it would make it even more difficult to refuse him.

"I assure you, Monsieur," she said coldly, "I am interested only because I find the Château so entrancing."

"That I understand," the Curator said quickly. "However, Mademoiselle, if you are really interested, there is so much you could do and so much that needs to be done."

He spoke so fervently that Drena found herself asking, "What exactly do you mean by that, Monsieur?"

The Curator looked towards the door as if he was afraid there might be somebody listening. Then he said in a low voice, "We want Monsieur le Duc to take a real interest in his home and care for the people who work for him. We want him to understand the difficulties of re-adjusting after the war, and most of all, to spend not only money, but also his time living at Saulieu."

"I thought ... he did ... live ... here," Drena said a little hesitatingly. She tried not to ask questions, but somehow they came to her lips before she could prevent them.

"He is here now at the Château for the first time in a year. It breaks my heart to see the rooms empty, the fires not lit, with only a handful of servants to keep it clean and for them to have wages that are long overdue."

He spoke as if he was saying what had been bottled up inside him for a long time. It seemed to burst forth as if he could no longer control it. Then he looked up at the picture over the mantelpiece and said, "If only he could have lived! Duc Francois was a great man and a good man, like his father and his grandfather before him. But he was guillotined, and those who took his place were not worthy of the name they bear."

Now he seemed almost to spit out the words and it made Drena feel uncomfortable. However, she thought how cleverly the Duc had managed to deceive both her and her Grandmother. He had spoken as if the house meant everything to him, and she had believed it when he had seemed deeply distressed by the damage which had not yet been repaired. But if the Curator was speaking the truth, the Duc did not really care at all for this magnificent building, preferring the gaieties of Paris and the entertainment to be found there.

It was difficult to know how to reply.

Then, as if he knew he had said too much, the old Curator pulled out the books of which he had been speaking from their shelves and gave them into her hands.

"I am an old man, Mademoiselle," he said in an apologetic tone, "and the old talk too much and feel too deeply. You must forgive me."

"There is nothing to forgive," Drena said, "and I am glad, very glad, Monsieur, that you love this beautiful place."

She turned and carried away the books. Without thinking, she made her way towards the main staircase, instead of the side one, down which she had come from her bed room. So she was half-way up the stairs when the Duc appeared at the top of them.

"Drena!" he exclaimed. "but you are not wearing a habit. Surely you are riding with me this morning?"

"I have been to borrow some books from the Library," Drena explained, "and as you did not mention it last night, I thought perhaps the horses were taking a rest."

"I bought the horses especially for you," the Duc replied, "and they will be very disappointed if they are forced to stay in their stables."

"Very well," Drena said. "I will go and change, but I hope some of the others are coming with us, so that we can have a race. It will be amusing to see if their horses can beat the ones we are riding."

She knew by the expression in the Duc's face that he realised she had no wish to go with him alone.

"I will tell Jules and Bernard to join us," he said, "but hurry, otherwise we will not wait for you."

Drena laughed. She was well aware that he had no intention of going without her. She hurried however to her room and changed quickly into her riding-habit.

Marie helped her, saying in the scolding voice of a Nanny, "Why didn't you wait for me, M'mselle, to dress you? That's what I'm here for."

"I did not expect to go riding this morning," Drena said, "but Monsieur le Duc insists that I do so."

"On the new horses that have just arrived, I suppose!" Marie said crossly. "The grooms were grumbling last night that there were new horses in the stable while they've not even been paid their wages for three months."

Drena did not answer. She only felt that all this information about the Duc was disturbing and unpleasant, and it would certainly distress her Grandmother if she learned of it.

"I am sure Grandmama believes every word he has said since we arrived here," Drena told herself, "but now I find that at least half of it is lies!"

One thing was very obvious and that was that the Duc needed money and needed it desperately. The question was, Drena thought as she went down the stairs, whether he would spend it on the Château and the people on the estate. Or would he more probably spend it extravagantly in Paris?

As she stepped out through the front door she saw that the Duc and his two cousins, Jules and Bernard, were already mounted and waiting for her. The magnificent horse she had ridden yesterday was being held by a groom, and as she appeared the two young men raised their hats and bade her good-morning.

The Duc merely looked at her with what she thought was a somewhat mocking smile on his thin lips.

"He knows that I am trying to avoid being alone with him," Drena thought, "but he is determined to have his own way."

She felt a pride and a strength she did not know she possessed seeping through her. Nevertheless she was still afraid that the trap was closing, and she would not be able to escape.

They all rode off together; the young men chatting and paying Drena compliments. At the same time, they were complaining about their horses.

"If we are going to race," one of them said, "it is extremely unfair seeing that our two horses are not as good as yours and Cousin Roger's."

"Then we will give you a start of two lengths," Drena offered.

"I will certainly accept that!" Jules exclaimed. "This old nag is nearly a hundred years old!"

"You insult me!" the Duc chimed in. "I have always owned good horse-flesh."

"Then where do you keep them, Cousin Roger?"

Jules asked. "In Paris? I hear they look very pretty trotting in the Bois with a lovely lady riding them!"

"Now you are being impertinent!" the Duc objected in a tone of thunder.

Jules looked embarrassed and knew he had gone too far. Instead of making excuses he pulled his horse away from the Duc's and deliberately rode ahead.

When they reached the level ground, the Duc arranged a race, with his two young cousins being given a generous start. Drena urged her horse forward, determined to win the race, if it was possible.

She and the Duc soon outpaced the two young men. They were racing as they had yesterday, neck and neck, and at a tremendous speed.

"I must beat him, I must!" Drena thought. She knew she was thinking not so much of the race, but of the Duc himself, yet as they neared the end of the field she was aware that by sheer expertise he was drawing ahead.

She made a last desperate effort, but there was no doubt that he had been the winner.

As she drew her horse to a standstill, he did the same and said, "I have won, Drena, as I always do, and always intend to do."

"Congratulations," she said, "on winning *the race*!"

She emphasised the last two words and the Duc said, "As I said, I am always the winner, whatever the contest!"

His meaning was so obvious that Drena turned away towards Jules and Bernard who had just joined them. "You did your best," she said, "but I agree with you that it was really not a fair contest. Tomorrow we will exchange horses, and then see if Monsieur le Duc is as successful!"

She sent him a defiant glance as she spoke. He did not reply and she had the feeling that he was laughing at her.

When they went back to the Château for breakfast, the Dowager Countess and several other members of the house-party were already in the Dining Room.

"You must tell me, Cousin Aimée," the Duc said as he sat down beside her, "what you would particularly like to see. There is a great deal more I have to show you."

"I think, actually, I would like to rest," the Dowager Countess said. "It is too hot to go driving, and I would prefer to sit in the shade and admire the beauty of the garden."

"Then that is what you shall do," the Duc replied as if he was conferring a great favour on her. "But I feel that your Granddaughter should see more of the estate, and I will take her driving in my phaeton."

"I am sure she will find that delightful!" the Dowager Countess said before Drena could speak.

The Duc looked at Drena expectantly, who said after a moment, "I think, as we have been riding, I will rest with Grandmama this morning, and perhaps we could go driving after luncheon."

The Duc made a gesture with his hands. "It shall be as you wish," he said. "You know that above all things, I want you to enjoy yourself here in my home which means so much to me."

Because she knew he was play-acting and lying, Drena did not look at him directly. She was afraid he would read the condemnation in her eyes. Instead she turned to talk to one of the relations who she realised was as anxious as the Duc was for her to marry in the family.

The Comtesse was middle-aged and, Drena learned, a widow. She said flattering things about the Duc, as if she was a young girl speaking of her lover. It made Drena realise that the Comtesse's clothes were out of date and well worn. She wore no jewellery.

Drena knew that, like everybody else in the Château, she was counting on her to restore the family fortunes. It seemed they were all hoping that when she married the Duc, they would each one of them benefit.

When the guests had finished breakfast they all went into the nearest Salon. But the Duc disappeared down the corridor which led to his Study.

A little later when Drena came from the Salon, she saw the Comtesse de Pastel going through a door. She had not appeared for breakfast and Drena guessed she had waited until she could have the Duc to herself.

When she thought about the Comtesse she wondered whether the magnificent emeralds she had been wearing last night have been given to her by her husband, or by the Duc. Would he really, in his present circumstances, spend so much money on women, rather than on the Château and those he employed?

She did not know the answer, but she was suspicious. She decided that the more she learned about the Duc, the more she despised him, but when she went out into the garden with the Dowager Countess she could talk of no one else.

"Roger is so charming," the Countess said, "and like all the Ducs of Saulieu, so handsome!" She paused before she asked, "Surely, ma petite, you find him different from those rather dull young Englishmen you have met?"

"He is certainly different, Grandmama!" Drena agreed, choosing her words with care. "At the same time, he is very interested in money."

"Of course he is!" the Dowager Countess answered. "You can see for yourself how much needs to be spent on restoring the Château to its former glory."

"I have heard, although I may be mistaken," Drena said tentatively, "that the Duc spends a great deal of his time in Paris."

The Dowager Countess smiled. "But naturally! Have you ever met a Frenchman who did not love Paris? The amusements to be found there draw them like a magnet."

"But . . . surely . . . Paris is . . . expensive?"

The Dowager Countess reached out her hand to pat her Granddaughter's. "All young men have to 'sow their wild oats', ma chérie, before they settle down to raise a family and become considerate husbands."

"The Duc is much older than my brother," Drena

said, "but Henry is already taking life very seriously, and preparing himself for when he will take over the estate."

"I am sure you will find when you drive with Roger," the Dowager Countess answered, "that he is deeply concerned with plans for planting more vines and cultivating the land which has been neglected during the war."

It was clear that her Grandmother would hear nothing against the Duc – instead Drena talked of the flowers and the fountains. She persuaded her Grandmother to tell her stories of when she was a small girl and lived at the Château.

When luncheon-time came, Drena was aware as she entered the hall that the Duc and the Comtesse de Pastel were just coming from the direction of the Study. It looked as if they had been together all the morning.

Drena thought it would be interesting to know what they had been discussing. She had no wish to be alone with the Duc and she therefore said when luncheon was over, "I do hope, Monsieur, you will forgive me, but I have a headache, and instead of going driving in this heat I really must go and lie down."

"A headache!" the Duc exclaimed. "Then of course I cannot submit you to driving in an open phaeton. Naturally, I am disappointed. I was looking forward to showing you the estate, and also having you *to myself.*"

The last two words were spoken in a very low voice,

but Drena was well aware of their meaning. "I know it is very tiresome of me," Drena said, "but I feel I must keep out of the sun."

She turned away before he could say any more and went up to her bedroom. The two books found for her by the Curator were waiting for her and she picked them up. Then she remembered there was another door in her room which led into a boudoir.

Marie had mentioned it to her, but she had not yet had time to explore. She opened the door and found it was a very attractive room, well furnished, with several vases of flowers on side-tables.

Drena thought perhaps it had been specially arranged so that she could be here alone. Or perhaps, she could sit with the Duc, so that they would not be disturbed.

She hesitated, then thought he was not likely to seek her out when she had said she had a headache, so she therefore settled herself down comfortably on the sofa. She arranged the silk cushions behind her and raised her legs. Opening one of the books she started to read.

It was a fascinating history of the Saulieus all down the centuries. She enjoyed every word and found that it ended in the 17th century. She hoped that the second book, which would take her into the 18th would be just as interesting.

Before she opened it, however, she thought she must stretch her legs, so she walked across the room to the window which overlooked the garden. The fountains were playing in the brilliant afternoon sunshine. The flowers seemed even more beautiful than they had been before. As she stood there she suddenly noticed two people coming from the shrubberies which were at the end of the lawn.

It was the Duc and the Comtesse de Pastel. The Comtesse's arm was linked through his. It was easy to see that they were talking intimately and animatedly to each other. "That is where the Duc's affections lie," Drena told herself, "and I would be very foolish to marry a man whose real interests are with another woman!"

As she watched them they turned into some bushes. She guessed that they were approaching the Château by a side path where they would not be seen.

"The sooner Grandmama and I go home, the better!" Drena told herself. She knew however that it was going to be very difficult to persuade her Grandmother that that was what she must do.

She came down later in the afternoon, and because she and her Grandmother had come from England tea was provided for them – something that did not normally happen at the Château.

"It is very kind of you to think of it," the Dowager Countess said to the Duc who had joined them. "Having lived in England for so long, I would miss my cup of tea at four-thirty if I did not have it."

"I knew that," the Duc said, "and that is why I thought of you and bought you the best tea available. I also told the Chef to make some *petits fours* which no one can resist!"

"You are so kind and considerate," the Dowager Countess murmured.

"I want to make you feel at home here," he said, "and that of course includes your very lovely and very charming Granddaughter."

He looked at Drena as he spoke.

With difficulty she prevented herself from asking him if he had enjoyed his afternoon. She told herself she must, on no account, upset her Grandmother. Not until the moment came when she told her that she wished to go home at any rate.

Drena hoped she could make her understand that in no circumstances would she marry the Duc. It was going to be difficult – very difficult – but somehow it had to be done.

There was a great deal of laughing and joking during tea. Then they all stayed talking until the Duc suggested that they had a glass of champagne before they went up to dress for dinner.

It certainly seemed to make the voices of the older relations rise. "It is years since I have seen a party like this in the Château," one of the elderly ladies murmured to Drena.

"But, surely, you come here very often?" Drena asked.

"I have not been here for the last five years," was the reply.

Then, as if she realised she had said something indiscreet, she said quickly, "That is what it seems, but of course I am just exaggerating!"

"They all tell lies!" Drena thought in disgust.

As she went up to her bedroom she told herself that the party was a charade, a theatrical performance in fact, put on to impress her and her Grandmother.

"It is despicable!" she told herself as she opened her bedroom door. "But how am I to make Grandmama understand what is happening here?"

CHAPTER FOUR

With some dexterity Drena avoided being alone with the Duc the whole evening. He tried to get her to go out into the garden with him to look at the stars. Then he suggested that he had something to show her in another room. But each time she managed to say "No".

She clung to her Grandmother, or made it clear that she would ask one of the cousins to go with them. Thus she was able to avoid what would have been a very uncomfortable conversation.

As she and her Grandmother went upstairs she realised it was still early, but the Dowager Countess was tired.

"I think it is the heat, ma petite," she explained, "and I do feel rather exhausted."

"You must rest, Grandmama," Drena said.

She went with her into her bedroom, kissed her goodnight, then left her with her lady's-maid.

In her own room she was about to ring the bell when she decided it was too hot for the moment to get into bed. Instead she decided she would read some more of the fascinating books she had borrowed from the Library. She went into the boudoir.

A fragrant perfume scented the air from the roses and the lilies arranged around the room. A small candelabrum on each side of the mantelpiece was lit and she lit another one beside the sofa. "I shall sit here and read my book," she decided. "Then when I am really tired, I will go to bed."

She was already half-way through the second volume of the history of the Ducs of Saulieu, which she found fascinating. She was deeply engrossed in the adventures of one of the Duchesses who was brave enough to go with her husband to sea, and had written home long letters about the storms they encountered and other experiences.

"I wonder what she looked like?" Drena asked herself.

Without really meaning to, she glanced around the room and realised there were several portraits of the Ducs and Duchesses. They were not large, and she thought that the larger pictures would have been too big to hide. They might therefore have been destroyed or taken away by the Revolutionaries.

She put down her book and rising to her feet started to look at the pictures on the walls. There was one which was very attractive and was really a large miniature painted on ivory and strangely enough the colours had hardly faded since it was done.

"I wonder if this is the Duchess of the story?" Drena questioned.

She lifted the portrait from the wall and turned it over. The Curator told her that he had written the names and dates of each of the family on the back of any picture there was of them. To her delight she had guessed right.

It was the Duchesse Thérèse about whom she had been reading, and she was just as beautiful as she had imagined she would be. Drena held the portrait in her hands for a long time, gazing at it. Then as she was about to put the picture back on the wall she realised the nail had become loose and was hanging forward.

"It must have been badly hung," Drena thought, "and if it had fallen to the floor, it could have been smashed."

She pulled at the nail, expecting it to come away in her hand. To her surprise, as she did so, the panelling behind it moved. For a moment she could not understand what was happening.

Then she realised that inadvertently she had stumbled upon one of the peep-holes referred to by the Curator. He had said they had been put there by one of the Ducs so that he could "eavesdrop" on conversations.

"I know the Curator will be pleased when I tell him what I have discovered," Drena thought. She pulled the nail free and as she did so the centre of the panelling opened. It was not large, only about three inches square and was exactly how she expected the Duc's peep-holes would look.

It was then she heard a voice.

A woman was speaking in French, saying, "I do wish you would hurry up, mon brave, and get this over."

Drena drew in her breath. She knew who it was who had spoken – it was the Comtesse de Pastel.

"I am doing my best," a man replied, "but the girl is determined to be elusive."

"I suppose she is playing 'hard to get'," the Comtesse said scornfully. "But hurry, hurry! I want the whole thing over, then we can be together."

Drena realised that she was speaking to the Duc and heard him reply, "We *will* be together, as soon as I can get hold of the money – that is all that matters!"

Listening, Drena felt as if she was turned to stone. Then she was aware, because the voices sounded so near, that the peep-hole opened onto the back of a bed. By looking through it she could see faintly there was a curtain, which hung between her and the two people on the other side of it.

It was such a shock that her first impulse was to shut the little panel and not listen to what they were saying. Then as she put down the portrait very gently on a chair beside her, she heard the Duc say, "If she goes on being difficult we shall have to try that drug of yours. You are quite certain it works?"

"I promise you, mon Cher, that it is very effective," the Comtesse replied. "It first makes those who take it rather limp and ready to do anything that is asked of them."

"In other words," the Duc said, "you have used it

on some of your admirers who were not as generous as you thought they should be."

The Comtesse gave a little laugh. "*Non, non,* you are not to ask questions! You know very well there is only one man in my life now – and that is you!"

She paused before she added, "But because that English girl is to be your wife, I would like to scratch out her eyes, or – kill her!"

"There is no need for you to do that," he replied. "She will die of an unfortunate accident as soon as I have my hands on her money. Then, ma chérie, my most adorable Eugénie, we can be together and enjoy ourselves."

There was a little silence, and Drena knew the Duc was kissing the Comtesse. Then he said, and his voice was deep and passionate, "I want you – God knows I want you! I cannot do without you. At the same time, we have to be sensible and dispose first of the two people who stand between us and the fortune we both need."

"Two?" the Comtesse enquired.

"But of course!" the Duc replied. "My Cousin Aimée has made a Will in favour of her Granddaughter. If Drena were to die first, she might leave her money to some other relative rather than to me."

The Comtesse gave a little scream. "I had not thought of that! Oh, clever, clever Roger – you think of everything!"

"I try to," he said, "and therefore both must die before we can be sure the money is ours."

"But you must be careful, very careful!" the

Comtesse warned. "If anyone should be suspicious..."

The Duc gave a little laugh. "They will not be suspicious at what I have planned. The lake is very deep and has a current which sucks down anyone who is in it. I was always warned about it as a child when I wanted to swim there."

"You mean – you will drown them both," the Comtesse said as if she was trying to understand exactly what he was planning.

"Both!" the Duc said. "It is very pleasant boating on the lake and the stream which feeds it. My mother found it most enjoyable, and I am sure my Cousin Aimée and my – wife – will not refuse my suggestion when I invite them to boat with me on the stream and into the lake itself."

He was speaking slowly, as if he was planning it all out and seeing it happen in his mind.

"That is clever, very clever!" the Comtesse agreed. "At the same time, you must be careful! No one must suspect for a moment that you are responsible in any way for losing them."

"I will make it very clear that I married Drena for love. Her Grandmother has already agreed that we shall be married as soon as possible, so that those I employ, as well as my relations, can enjoy the festivities that I will give as the Duc de Saulieu."

He gave a little chuckle as he said, "It will be a magnificent display, including the best fireworks that have ever been seen in this part of France. But you, my lovely one, must not be present."

"I cannot... leave you!" the Comtesse cried. "How can I go away and leave you when you have so many problems to face?"

"The problems will all have been solved from the moment I marry Drena," the Duc said, "and my lovely Siren, who mesmerises me, must not prevent me from doing my duty as Bridegroom!"

He laughed again, and it was an ugly sound. "It will be hard enough to tell her I love her, even if you are not in the next room. My wedding would be an excruciating agony, if I knew I could so easily be with you."

"That is what I wanted you to say," the Comtesse said. "Oh, Roger, Roger, I love you, but I cannot be away from you for long."

"It will be only as long as it takes to make me a millionaire by marriage and then to dispose of my wife by the means I have just explained. Then I shall be free to marry you."

The Comtesse made a sound that was almost a shriek. "You have asked me! You have asked me! Oh, Roger – I have been waiting for the moment when you would ask me to be your wife, and thought it would never come!"

"Do you think I would leave you free to look at any other man?" the Duc asked. "You are mine, Eugénie, and I will kill any man in whom you are interested, just as I am prepared to kill two women to make you happy and give you the jewels I promised you."

The Comtesse did not reply, and Drena knew that once again they were kissing each other. Very quietly, with hands that trembled, she shut the panel and tip-toed across the room, blowing out the candles one by one, went into her bedroom.

She walked to the bed and sat on it, feeling as if her legs would no longer support her. Was it possible that she had heard such an appalling plot being described in the next room?. Only because one of the Ducs de Saulieu had been eccentric enough to make listening-holes in many parts of the Château she now knew the truth. There was no question of it just being a nightmare from which she could not awake. Then she realised that she had to do something about it.

Her first thought was that she must tell her Grandmother. Then an inner voice told her this was unwise, because the Dowager Countess would not believe her. But if she remained in the Château she knew she would be drugged by something that was put into her food, or else into what she drank.

Then she would acquiesce in everything the Duc wanted.

Because she had read so extensively, she knew about certain drugs which came from the East. They could affect people in any way the 'Provider' desired. She would take the drug unawares and after that she would lose her willpower and be a puppet in the Duc's hands.

She knew now why instinctively she had been afraid of him since the first moment she had touched his hand. For the same reason, her dislike of him had increased every moment she was in contact with him.

"I must get away . . . I must . . . return to England!" she told herself.

Then she knew that the Duc would never willingly let her escape. He wanted her money, and he would contrive to have it by fair means or foul. She could think of nothing she could do to stop him. She put a hand up to her forehead. Then as if they drew her to them, she went to the window to look up at the stars. She pulled back the curtains, opened the casements and prayed.

She prayed fervently with a fear which increased every moment as she realised how helpless she was. "Save me! Save me!" she whispered. "And save Grandmama too. Tell me . . . what to . . . do!"

She was praying both to God and her mother. Suddenly, as if they were speaking to her, she knew the answer.

She went to the *secrétaire* which stood in a corner of her bed-room. It was so old and valuable that she thought it must have been one of the articles they had managed to hide from the rioting Revolutionaarikes.

She sat down and wrote two letters. One was to her Grandmother, which took a little time because she thought about and considered every sentence. Finally she wrote:

"Dearest Grandmama,
 I know you will understand that I must have a little time to think before I accept, as you want me to, the Duc as my future husband.
 I have just remembered that I have some friends

who live only a short distance from here, and I am going to stay with them for two or three days.

When I return I hope I can give the Duc the answer you want me to, but I must think about it very carefully, and of course pray that I am doing the right thing.

Please, Dearest Grandmama, do not be angry with me, and I will be back almost as soon as you realise I have gone!

I am
>Your most devoted and
>loving granddaughter,
>>Drena."

She addressed the letter to her Grandmother and put it in a prominent position on the *secrétaire*.

Then hurriedly she wrote another letter, to Sir Matthew Hill, who was the Senior Partner of the firm of Solicitors with whom her Grandmother and her Father dealt. She wrote saying that he would think it incredible, but she and her Grandmother were in a desperately dangerous situation where they might both be murdered.

She asked him to come to Burgundy immediately and to contact her where she was staying at . . .

She left a space, and went on:

"I think it best that you do not worry Papa with this, but bring with you a man who is both trustworthy and strong, and on whom you can rely if things become more unpleasant than they are at the moment.

I will explain to you the moment you arrive what is happening, and I beg you to believe me that it is very serious. I do not exaggerate when I say that we are in grave danger . . ."

She signed it, but did not seal the letter down. She knew she had to add an address where Sir Matthew could find her, but for the moment she had no idea where that might be.

She was still shaking from the shock she had received, but she forced herself to lie down quietly on her bed. There was no possibility of her going to sleep, for there was a great deal to do before tomorrow dawned.

It was four o'clock in the morning.

Wearing one of her pretty riding-habits and carrying a bundle over her arm, Drena tip-toed along the corridor. She went down a side-staircase which led her to the back of the Château. Everything was very quiet and the few servants there were in the house were asleep.

She let herself out just as the stars were beginning to fade a little in the sky, but there was not yet the glimmer of the dawn.

Going to the stables, she found, as she expected, there was only one groom on duty. He was a youth of about sixteen years of age, and he was fast asleep on a pile of straw. She woke him gently, just touching his shoulder, and saying, "Wake up! I need your help!"

He opened his eyes and stared at her in astonishment.

"It is all right," Drena said softly, "but I want you to help me saddle one of the horses. I am finding it hard to sleep and so I am taking a little exercise."

The lad yawned and rubbed his eyes with the back of his hand as he went into one of the stalls.

Drena thought it would be a mistake to take with her either of the new horses which she and the Duc had ridden. They would be too conspicuous; and anyone noticing her would wonder where it came from.

Instead she took the better of the two horses which Bernard and Jules had disparaged. The one she chose was a sturdy animal which she knew would carry her a long way before getting tired.

She climbed onto the mounting-block to get into the saddle, then she rode off while the young groom was still yawning. She was sure the minute she was out of sight he would go back to his pile of straw and fall asleep again.

She had no idea where to go, but thought, however, it should be northwards, so as to be nearer to England when Sir Matthew came out to find her. She had known him ever since she was a child, and she was certain he would take her letter seriously and not think it was some kind of joke which he could ignore.

She rode away, having tied her bundle to the back of the saddle, and she wondered as she did so if she would really be able to look after herself until Sir Matthew joined her.

It was encouraging to know she had some money

with her, for before they had set out on their journey to France the Dowager Countess had given her the equivalent of thirty pounds in Francs.

"I shall not need all that, Grandmama!" she had expostulated.

"You will need to tip handsomely when we reach the Château," the Dowager Countess had replied, "and it would be embarrassing for you to have to come to me for every penny you want to spend."

"Thank you, thank you!" Drena said. "It is very kind of you. I have never before had so much money in my hand all at one time!"

She gave a little laugh before she added, "Papa gives me my pocket-money every week, but it is not a very large amount."

"As my heir," the Dowager Countess said, "you will have to learn to handle money. You must also realise, ma chérie, that people will expect you to be generous."

She gave a little sigh as she added with a twinkle in her eye, "I do not believe there is a Charity in the whole of England to which I have not been invited to subscribe!"

Drena laughed too. She thought now how lucky it was that at least she would not starve before Sir Matthew arrived. She could also stay, if necessary, at an Inn or an Hotel, though she had a feeling however that that might be dangerous.

She was not so foolish as not to realise that she looked very different from any ordinary young Frenchwoman who might be travelling about the country alone, but she had not dared to take one of the Duc's grooms with her.

All she had to do, she reassured herself, was to hide somewhere until Sir Matthew arrived, even though it might have to be in a wood or under a hedge. Anywhere, in fact, as long as she was not drugged and dragged ignominiously to the altar.

She rode over the land which she knew belonged to the Duc. She could see for herself it was very neglected. What grapevines there were looked overgrown, others had withered away for lack of attention.

There were hamlets as bad, if not worse, than those she had seen at Saulieu. She tried not to think of how the Duc had deliberately shown them to her to evoke her sympathy. In reality, he intended to spend her money, when he had it, in Paris.

"He is more wicked than anyone could imagine a man could be!" she told herself. Then she shivered as she recalled what she had overheard last night.

The Curator had told her about the listening-holes, and that he had put the names and dates on the back of the portraits. Had he not done so, she would not have overheard the Duc's wicked plans for her and her Grandmother. "My Guardian Angel must be watching over me," she thought as she rode on.

As she stopped to water her horse at a stream she realised she was hungry. At the same time she was still quite near the Château, so she did not dare to stop at an Inn or even buy food from a shop. She was sure the Duc would instigate a search for her, especially if he was suspicious of her story of staying with friends in the vicinity.

It would not take long for him to learn that an elegant young woman in a smart riding-habit had ridden by alone. She must therefore keep to the fields in order to avoid as far as possible any human habitation. But as the day wore on she realised that her horse was beginning to flag, and she herself was both hungry and thirsty.

It was then she saw ahead of her what looked like a church or a chapel. As she drew nearer she saw there were a number of gravestones just in front of the church door.

The door itself was open. That meant it had not been damaged, or had been restored so that those living nearby could continue to use it. Reaching the gate of the small graveyard, Drena dismounted, and put the reins over one of the spikes on the iron gate.

Then she walked up the paved footpath and through the porch-door of the little church, which was very small and untidy, but obviously still in use. There was an altar on which stood a Cross, and also two vases filled with fresh flowers. The walls of the Chapel were rough and in need of repair but there was a statue of Joan of Arc and also one of St. Anthony.

Drena looked up at him now and said in her heart, "Please, St. Anthony, find me someone to help me."

As if St. Anthony answered her immediately, an old Priest came through a door at the end of the Chancel. He was wearing a black cassock, and he genuflected as he faced the altar, before he started to walk down the aisle towards her. As he drew nearer she saw that he was a very old man with white hair, wearing spectacles, with one of the lenses being darkened as if he could not use that eye.

As he reached her Drena said, "Good-afternoon, Father! I have come here because I need your help."

The Priest looked at her with his good eye. She realised that until she spoke he had not been aware of her presence. "Of course, my daughter," he said kindly, "I will help you if I can."

He indicated with his hand some rather battered chairs which were arranged at the back of the Chapel behind two pews which were in need of repair. He sat down and as Drena joined him he said, "I am afraid I have no Confessional here at the moment, but I am having one made as soon as we can afford it."

Drena smiled. "I do not need a Confessional at the moment, Father. What I seek is sanctuary."

"Sanctuary?" the Priest repeated in surprise.

"Yes, Father, I am in great danger," Drena explained. "There is a man who wishes to marry me and is prepared to use every method he can to make me accept him — even threatening to drug me!"

"That is of course very wrong — very wrong!" the Priest said.

"I know it is, Father, and that is why I am begging you, if it is possible, to shelter me, or at least tell me where I can hide until help can reach me."

"You are alone?" the Priest asked.

"Alone, except for the horse on which I escaped

from where I was staying," Drena said, "and it is very important that as few people as possible should know that I am here."

She paused before she went on, "When I saw your Church and that the door was open, I felt as if God was telling me this was where I would be safe."

"And God always knows best," the Priest said. "So I will do all I can to help you."

"Thank you, Father," Drena said with a sigh of relief, "and I am ready to do anything I can in return for your help."

"I am thinking," the Priest said, "that we are desperately in need of somebody at the moment to help with the orphans who we have put, for want of somewhere better, in the House to which this Chapel belongs."

"Then of course I will help with them," Drena said quickly. "I love children, and I expect you have someone who will tell me in what way I can be of any assistance in looking after them."

The Priest gave a little laugh. "I think they will tell you that themselves. They are good children, but they need to eat and play, as all children do, and it is very difficult when the woman who is in charge of them is unwell."

"Then of course I will do anything that is required of me," Drena smiled.

The Priest was looking at her and, she knew, was taking in every detail of her appearance. She was aware it contrasted with the shabbiness of his cassock and with the chapel itself.

"I think," the Priest said after a moment, "you had

better stay not at the Orphanage, but at my house, where my Housekeeper can act as your chaperone."

Drena almost smiled at the idea. Then she knew in actual fact that he was being sensible. Of course, looking as she did, she would need a chaperon, or else the village people would be talking about her.

"Thank you, Father, thank you very much!" she said. "I am very grateful, and perhaps I can help your Housekeeper as well, and brush out the Chapel for you." She had been aware as she was talking that the floor was dusty and that leaves had blown in from outside.

"That is certainly something that wants doing!" the Priest agreed.

He rose to his feet, but Drena said, "There is one more thing, Father – I can pay for my accommodation and my food. I have some money with me."

"That is unnecessary," the Priest said. "you are my guest."

"Thank you very much for giving me shelter, Father," Drena said. "I prayed as I came into the Church, and now I feel I must thank God and St. Anthony for your kindness."

"God will receive your thanks," the Priest said with a smile. "Now we will eat, but before we do so, I will bless you, my child."

CHAPTER FIVE

When Drena rose from her knees, the Priest said, "Come along now, my child, and I will take you to my house. But perhaps first we should introduce ourselves. My name is Father Jean."

"And I am . . . Drena . . ." she began.

She thought swiftly that to give him her own name could be very dangerous for if she gave him a name that was English it might cause gossip and speculation. After a little pause she continued, "I am, as it happens, a very unimportant and distant relation of the Duc of Saulieu."

The Priest did not seem surprised. He simply said, "Then you have certainly come home."

Drena looked at him in astonishment. "Home?" she asked. "I do not . . . understand."

"This is the village of Fabrey and if you are a member of the family you will be aware that the old

Duchesse of Saulieu had a Château here."

"No, I ... did not ... know that," Drena said, wondering if she had made a terrible mistake.

"It is where we have now housed the orphans," Father Jean explained, "because it has not been lived in since the Revolution."

He walked towards the door as he spoke. When they reached the Churchyard, he saw Drena's horse. "You must bring him to my stable," he said, "though it is only a small one. You could if you wish put him in the stables of the Château, or there is a paddock in which he would be quite safe."

Drena smiled. "Your stable sounds the most convenient, and I have ridden a long way."

They walked down the road, Drena leading the horse.

A few minutes later she saw in front of them a little house. The Priest led the way through a gate but, instead of taking the brick path to the front door, he took another one which led to a shed attached to the side of the house. It was large enough to house two horses, but it was empty. As if Drena had asked the question Father Jean said, "I have no horse of my own, but when people come to see me they stable their horses here."

There was fresh straw on the floor, a bucket of water, and some hay in the manger. Drena thought, as she unsaddled her horse, he would be very comfortable there.

Father Jean did not offer to help her, but waited until she had finished. Then he took her back the way they had come to the path which led up to the front door of the house.

He opened the door, saying as he did so, "The Duchesse Alise was only in late middle-age when she left the great Château in Saulieu, and came here where she spent her last years."

He paused and then continued, "She wanted to give her son a chance to be on his own and during her life she was loved by everyone here in the village."

Drena gave a little cry. "The Duchesse Alise? Was her son the Duc François de Saulieu?"

"Yes, he was," Father Jean affirmed. "He was a very wonderful man. I am sure he is missed not only in Saulieu, but also in the whole of Burgundy."

"He was ... guillotined," Drena said in a low voice.

"That is right," the Priest agreed. "They took him from here to Dijon and there he lost his life."

Drena thought it was very strange. Of all places in Burgundy she had by chance come to one where the Saulieu family had a Château. Then she told herself there were so many of the family that no one would be particularly interested in hearing that yet another Saulieu had arrived in Fabrey.

If the Duc *was* looking for her, any other name might arouse his suspicions. She had a feeling that her Guardian Angel was helping her, and if she stayed in this very small hamlet until Sir Matthew arrived, she would be safe. "I have an important letter to go to England," she said as they walked into the Priest's house. "Could you please give me your exact address, so that the person to whom I am writing can reply?"

"Of course," Father Jean said. "A letter will find you if your friend just addresses it: "The Priest's House, Fabrey, Burgundy."

"Thank you," Drena said. "I will do that, if I may?"

"The original Priest's house," Father Jean explained, "was burned down by the Revolutionaries. It was fortunate that they did not also destroy the Church. They were in fact so excited at finding the Duc himself at the Château that they did very little damage."

"I cannot bear to think of all the beautiful things that were destroyed," Drena said.

"We all feel like that about the things which are sacred or dear to us," the Priest replied.

Then he was calling out, "Madame Muate! I am back!"

"That is good," a voice said from the back of the house. "Your supper's ready!"

"We have a guest," Father Jean added.

There was no reply, but Drena thought, although she might have been imagining things, that the woman to whom he was talking groaned.

The Priest opened the door of a cosy little Dining Room, where the table could seat only four people and there were four chairs. She thought that Father Jean had to be very restricted in the number of guests he entertained. The table was already laid, and the Priest pointed to a chair that was near to where he was obviously expected to sit.

"Madame Muate will look after you," he said. "She is a very good cook, but like me she is growing old and finds even this small house is too much for her."

"Then of course I will help her while I am here," Drena said. "Shall I go to the kitchen now and offer to bring in the food?"

"I thinks perhaps you should wait until you have been introduced," the Priest answered.

As he spoke the door opened. An elderly woman with grey hair and a thin, anxious face came in carrying a tray.

"Another guest, father?" she asked in an accusing voice. "You did not warn me!"

"I did not know myself that a member of the Saulieu family would be honouring us with her company."

The elderly woman put down the tray on the table. "A Saulieu!" she said. "There are so many of them in this part of the world that I have ceased counting."

Drena laughed. "I can only apologise, Madame, for arriving unexpectedly. As Father Jean will explain, I have come to him for help."

"Who ever does anything else?" Madame Muate asked.

Drena saw she had brought in a tray with a plate, knives and forks which she put down in front of her. "I expect you are hungry," she said. "It is lucky that tonight I have a fat rabbit for the Father's supper."

"It sounds delicious," Drena said.

And in fact it was.

Afterwards there was a suet pudding with a treacle sauce that Drena remembered having as a child. She thought that perhaps, because the Priest was so poor, Madame Muate filled him up with starchy foods.

When the frugal meal was over the Priest excused himself and rose from the table, Drena said, "I will help Madame Muate by taking the plates into the kitchen. Then perhaps, Father, I can join you later."

The Priest smiled. "I can see you are a kind and helpful girl," he said, "so we will wait for tomorrow to tell you about the orphans. Go and help Madame. She will appreciate it."

Drena did as she was told and Madame said, "If you are going to help me, I hope you have something more practical to wear than that smart habit you have on!"

Drena had carried in the bundle she had attached to the saddle from the stable, and had put it down in the hall. "I have only two gowns," she answered, "which I was able to carry on the back of my saddle."

"And where are you going in such a hurry?" Madame asked.

"I have come here for sanctuary," Drena explained. "I am running away from danger and I have asked the Father to hide me until someone to whom I have written in England can arrive here."

Madame Muate looked astonished. "From England?" she repeated.

"I am very anxious to get in touch with him as quickly as possible," Drena said, "and I want to post a letter to him tonight. I have only to add the address of where I am staying."

"The grocer will take the letters, and he is quite

near," Madame Muate replied. "If your letter is urgent I will take it to him tonight."

"I would be very grateful if you could," Drena said, "but, please, do not tell the grocer that I am here."

She thought for a moment, then added, "If you must, perhaps you could say that I am one of the Saulieu family who has come to look at the Château of the Duchesse Alise."

"There have been quite a number of them doing that from time to time," Madame Muate replied, "and the grocer will not be surprised if there is another."

"Thank you, thank you," Drena said. "You are very kind, and it is of the utmost importance that no one should know where I am."

Madame Muate's eyes twinkled. "If they saw you looking as you do now," she said, "it would be difficult for them not to look again!"

"I will just stay in the house with you," Drena said, "and help the orphans in the Château, as Father Jean has asked me to do."

She appreciated that Madame Muate did not press her for any more details, but took her upstairs. There were only four bedrooms in the house, but the two reserved for guests were very small. In Drena's room there was an iron bedstead, one small rug on the floor, a hard chair and a wash-hand-stand.

She did not say anything, but she must have looked surprised, for Madame Muate said, "I expect Father Jean told you that the Priest's House was burned down in the Revolution and everything he possessed with it."

"He was here at the time?" Drena asked.

"He was a young man then. We were all delighted to have him because he seemed to galvanize the village into doing things they had never done before."

She sighed. "But when the Revolutionaries came," she went on, "he had to hide, and after they had gone he held Services in secret, always frightened that those cruel men would come back and destroy the Church."

It was obvious from the way she spoke that what they had suffered during the Revolution was still very in her mind. "And during the war," Madame Muate continued, "we were poorer than ever, since the men working in the fields were all taken from us. I have often wondered how it is that we are still alive!"

"There is one thing I want to tell you," Drena said quickly, "which is that I can afford to pay for being here."

Madame Muate shook her head. "I am sure Father Jean would not hear of it! He would share his last crust with anyone who turned to him for help."

"I thought you might say that, Madame," Drena said, "so we will have to be very clever. I will give you some money – I promise you I can afford it – and with it you can buy good food for the Father and for . . . us."

"You really mean you can afford it?" Madame asked. "The Father would be very angry if he thought I was depriving you."

"I promise you on the Bible that I am quite well off, and I cannot possibly let Father Jean or yourself suffer because I have foisted myself upon you."

She took from her pocket as she spoke a small bundle of French francs and gave them into Madame Muate's hand. There was the equivalent of five English pounds. Madame Muate looked at them in astonishment and said "All this? I can buy a Lucullan feast with a tenth of that!"

"You must spend what you think is right," Drena said, "and when that is finished, I have some more."

She had in fact divided her money so that it was in several pockets in case anyone should be suspicious that she had so much with her.

Madame Muate was still staring at the money. Then she said, "The Father will bless you for this, Mademoiselle, and I thank you from the bottom of my heart"!

Briskly, as if she was ashamed of showing her emotions, she fetched some clean sheets and pillowcases. Drena helped her make the bed, and when they had finished she went downstairs to say goodnight to Father Jean.

He was sitting at a desk in what she realised was his Study. It was as sparsely furnished as the rest of the house. There was a sofa that was on its last legs and badly in need of re-upholstering, and there were also two dilapidated, but comfortable, armchairs. Only one small rug was on the floor, and the curtains barely covered the windows.

But as Father Jean smiled at her she had the feeling that she was safe. "I am going to bed now, Father," she said, "because it has been a long day, and I am tired. But I want to thank you more than I can put into words for your kindness to me. I know that it must have been God Himself who led me to Fabrey."

She saw the Priest was pleased at the way she spoke.

"Go to bed, my child," he said, "and God be with you. We need never be afraid as long as we turn to Him for protection."

When Drena was upstairs in her room she said a fervent prayer of thankfulness before she got into bed. How could she have been so lucky, she asked herself, as to find somebody like Father Jean?

He had accepted her without any explanation of why she was there, nor had he cross-examined her as to what she was doing.

She knew that Madame Muate would post the letter she had left on the kitchen table, and she could only pray that Sir Matthew would come as quickly as he possibly could. In the meantime she knew the wicked Duc would not dispose of her Grandmother until she returned and married him.

When she got into bed she realised not only how tired she was, but she was also a little stiff from riding for so long. It was very quiet, except that far away in the distance she could hear an owl hooting. As she listened, her eyes closed and she fell asleep.

In the morning, Drena put on one of the gowns she had brought with her which was comparatively simple. But it looked very elegant and far too *chic* to be worn in such a small village. There was however nothing she could do about it.

As if Madame realised her predicament, she said when she went downstairs, "If you are going to help me with the breakfast, there is an apron hanging beside the door which you can put over that pretty frock."

It was a large, enveloping apron, and once it was on, Drena knew that she looked much more practical and businesslike in it.

Father Jean had already gone to the Church to say morning prayers. When he returned Drena and Madame Muate had prepared his breakfast, with two eggs and bacon for each of them.

Drena had the idea that because Madame Muate could now afford it, the eggs need not be made to last for longer than one day.

There were also some croissants baked with a lightness which only the French could achieve. A large pat of butter and a new honeycomb were there to spread on them.

"Where have all these good things come from?" Father Jean asked as he sat down at the table.

"'Ask no questions and you will be told no lies!'" Madame Muate replied. "We have a guest — a very pretty guest — and we cannot allow her to starve."

The Priest chuckled, but he made no further protests and merely enjoyed his breakfast.

When he had finished he said, "Now, child, I will take you to the Orphanage. Then, as I have some people to see in the village, you can come back here and help Madame."

"I would like to do that," Drena said.

She had nothing to put on her head except her riding-hat, which she thought would look incongruous and far too smart. She therefore put a silk scarf that she had brought with her over her head, and kept her apron on. The Priest did not say anything yet she had the idea that his eyes twinkled when he looked at her.

They set off to walk past the Church and into the garden of the Château. There were thick shrubs, then further on a rock garden. Then they came to what had been a lawn. Because it had not been tended it now resembled a hay-field, but there were flowers peeping through the grass, and creepers which had grown wildly up the trees and over the bushes. Gold honeysuckle and several overgrown shrubs were in blossom.

It was untidy, but at the same time it looked enchanting.

Ahead of them Drena could see the Château that had belonged to the Duchesse Alise. It too was very attractive with little turrets on each side, and a portico over the front door. But as they drew nearer, Drena could see that slates were missing from the roof and many of the windows were cracked.

"You say that no one has lived here since the Duchesse Alise?" she asked. She was thinking as she spoke how beautiful the Duchesse had looked in the large miniature that she had found on the wall of her boudoir.

"I think the family have forgotten about this Château," the Father replied, "but of course, the present Duc is not interested in Burgundy nor in his great estate, and spends his time in Paris."

"How do you know that?" Drena asked curiously.

"Gossip flies on the wind," Father Jean replied, "and people talk, wherever they live, of those who should protect and care for them."

Drena knew that the Duc was not interested in his property. She wondered what Father Jean would say if she told him that the Duc intended to kill her. She told herself however that that must remain a secret until Sir Matthew arrived.

Like the Priest's house, the Château, when they entered it, was very sparsely furnished. But the family portraits were still hanging on the walls and were very beautiful. Some of the ceilings were painted and the mantelpieces sculpted.

"This house must have been very impressive when the Duchesse Alise was alive," Drena remarked.

"It was indeed!" Father Jean agreed. "but over the years, because the house has been unoccupied, everything that was left was gradually stolen."

He sighed, then continued, "I have learned to shut my eyes when I see carpets and curtains in some of the cottages which I know have come from here."

"And when did the orphans come?" Drena enquired.

"Only two years ago when we had no idea what to do with them. There are so many children in France whose fathers have been killed, and their mothers have either died from overwork or in some cases have abandoned them, because they could not face seeing their children starve, and had no man to look after them."

The Priest spoke in a practical manner. It was as if he was not condemning them, but understood why they had behaved as they had.

As they crossed the hall there was the sound of young voices. The Priest opened what must once have been the door to the Drawing Room which overlooked the garden at the back of the Château. Now it was practically empty, except for a few hard chairs.

The orphans were playing amongst themselves. Some of them were quite well dressed, but the majority were in clothes there were little more than rags. When they saw the Priest they jumped up and ran towards him.

"Father Jean! Father Jean!" they were shouting.

"Look at what I have made!"

"Look what that naughty boy Jacques has done to me!"

They all talked at once: "Look at this!" "Look at that!" "Listen, Father . . .!"

The Priest moved amongst them, patting one on the head, another on the shoulder, and smiling at them as if he loved them all, good or bad. "I have brought this lady to see you," he said, "and she has lots of stories to tell you which I know you will enjoy."

He looked at Drena as he spoke with a smile as if he was deliberately challenging her.

"A story – tell us a story!"

"I will do my best," she said, "and I hope you will not be disappointed."

"Most of them cannot read," the Priest said in a low voice.

She knew then why he had said she would tell them stories. Looking round the room she realised there were no bookcases, and she supposed therefore there were no books. She could not help thinking of the huge Library at the Château in Saulieu, and it had obviously not occurred to the Duc that the children in Burgundy needed education: teachers, books and other things which only he could provide. Even if he did have any money, she knew it would be spent in Paris and not on poor children like these.

She was talking to them and asking their names when the woman who was in charge of them came in.

She was over fifty and looked anxious and troubled. "It is nice to see you, Father," she said when she reached him, "but another ceiling has fallen in during the night, and there is nothing I can do about it."

"I have brought someone who will come and help you when she is not helping me," Father Jean said. "This is Mademoiselle Drena, who arrived to stay with me unexpectedly last night."

The woman, whom he introduced as Mademoiselle Alesia, shook hands somewhat indifferently with Drena. But she did say she gladly welcomed any help however small it might be. When the Father had left she said to Drena, "They keep bringing me more orphans, but we have no money to feed those we have already. It is a disgrace that no one has any care for us or understands that children, however unwanted they may be, have to eat."

Because she was obviously worrying, Drena gave her the same amount of money that she had given to Madame Muate.

Mademoiselle Alesia asked the same question, "Can you really afford all this, Mademoiselle? I can hardly believe my eyes! I have been asking and praying for money, but not a penny has come for over two weeks!"

"Where does your money come from?" Drena asked.

"It is supposed to come from Monsieur le Maire and those who administer the Département in Dijon. But there are so many other calls on them that they just have not the funds to go round."

She shrugged her shoulders. "Or that is what they tell me. If it was not that the people in the village take pity on us and bring me potatoes and turnips from their gardens, these children would be starving!"

She looked at Drena anxiously as she said, "Am I really to spend all this on them. I am sure I can make it last a long time!"

"Spend it, spend it so that they no longer feel hungry," Drena urged. "I will try somehow to let you have some more."

She thought that even when she got back to England she would send them money. She was sure her Grandmother would give her anything she asked for these children, for she knew as she looked at them that they were far too thin and too pale through not having the right food, or enough of it.

Some of the little girls were very pretty. Yet once the excitement of her appearance died down they were sitting limply on the floor. They were not playing — just too tired, or too hungry, to move about.

"Would you like me to help you cook the luncheon?" she asked, "or shall I amuse the children?"

"I will cook the luncheon," Mademoiselle Alesia replied, "if you will stay here while I run down to the butcher's. With what you have given me, Mademoiselle, they shall have a feast!"

Drena smiled and went back into the Drawing Room. The children gathered round her and she started a story. It was one she had read herself as a child, and she elaborated on it with little anecdotes of things she had done herself, so that it made the heroine seem far more adventurous than she had been in the original tale.

The children listened with rapt attention which Drena found very moving. When she finished one story she went on with another. Her voice was getting hoarse when finally the door opened and Mademoiselle Alesia said in a tone of triumph, "Luncheon is ready! You are in for a big surprise!"

The children got to their feet and ran to the adjacent room which had originally been the Dining Room. Several tables had been pushed together, but there were no tablecloths. As the children came in they each collected a bowl in which they would have their food from a side-table near the door. Then as they saw the end of the table on which there was a huge leg of lamb they gave cries of excitement.

There was not only lamb. As if Mademoiselle Alesia was determined to do them proud, there were some small sausages to go with it. And she had made a sauce with mushrooms of a type that was only obtainable in France.

Mademoiselle carved the lamb into equal portions for each, and when she had done so, there was very little left. But the children ate everything that was put in front of them. Then they scraped their bowls of the last vestiges of potatoes and turnips which she had also cooked.

Mademoiselle Alesia looked round at them and said, "And now, because this kind lady is here, we are going to have a special treat."

"More?" several of the children asked.

"Yes, more!" Mademoiselle Alesia replied.

She carried away the bare leg-bone of the lamb, and shortly came back with a dish that made them all gasp before they started to clap their hands.

It was a huge chocolate soufflé with hot chocolate running over it and smelling delicious. The children were so thrilled that Drena felt the tears come into her eyes. She thought she had never seen children look so happy and, as she thought to herself, at so little cost.

How could the Duc spend what money he had in giving jewels to Madame Eugénie?

How could he allow little children like these to starve?

"He is cruel and horrible in every way," Drena told herself.

Suddenly she remembered that she was escaping from him, and gave an involuntary shiver.

During the next two days Drena was very busy. She hardly had time to think about herself, or the difficulties that lay ahead. She helped at the Priest's house in the mornings, and in the afternoon she went to the Orphanage to play with the children, and to arrange games for them in the garden.

She was considering that when they got a little stronger that they might have a paperchase.

But what they really enjoyed, more than anything else, was to sit round her and listen to her telling them stories. These became more and more fantastic as each day went by.

After Drena had been there for a few days she gave Mademoiselle Alesia another five pounds. At least the children had one decent meal every day, though she knew she must not run out of money before Sir Matthew arrived. But it was extraordinary how much both Madame Muate and Mademoiselle Alesia could buy for a few centimes in the local shops.

When Saturday came, Drena decided to clean up the Church. She remembered how dusty and dirty it had looked when she first arrived, and she hoped that when Father Jean said Mass on Sunday it would look very different.

She began by cleaning the brass Cross which stood on the altar. Then she dusted the candlesticks, which were also made of brass. After that she brushed out the Nave. She pushed the seats to one side so that she could remove the dirt that had accumulated over the years out through the front door. "Surely," she was thinking, "there is somebody in the village who would paint the inside walls. And the altar-cloths are torn and should be mended."

Then she remembered that the women had to struggle just to keep alive. The majority of the people only had to eat what they grew themselves. The men who had come back from the war were nearly all crippled and of little help. Indeed one man had been blinded, another had lost an arm, another a leg.

There was no school and the children played in the road. When they heard what was happening at the Orphanage they begged to be allowed to join in. They listened to the stories that Drena told, and she was thinking now as she brushed out the dirt about what she would tell them to-morrow.

She had suggested that on Sunday they should have a day of rest, but they had however protested fervently that they wanted her to come and talk to them as before.

She was wondering if now they might absorb a little history lesson instead of hearing of fairies, giants and dragons. A history lesson would be appropriate, but she was not sure if she knew enough about French Kings to make it into a story.

Deep in her thoughts, she suddenly became aware of footsteps. Glancing up she saw a man entering the Church. He was tall and broad-shouldered, and when she looked at him Drena had the feeling that she had seen him somewhere before. Then she felt afraid that he might be someone from Saulieu who had come to discover where she was.

The man stood still when he saw her.

She was sure from his appearance that he was a Gentleman. He was obviously rich, or at least rich enough to afford very smart, well-fitting clothes. His cravat was tied in a most intricate fashion with the points of his collar high above his jawline.

"*Bonjour, Mademoiselle!*" he said.

After he had spoken, Drena saw that he was staring at her, it seemed, in astonishment. She was frightened.

She had no idea how unexpectedly beautiful she looked in the light of the sun coming through the stained-glass window over the altar. "*Bonjour, Monsieur,*" she replied. Despite herself her voice trembled.

"I should be very grateful," the newcomer said, "if I could see the Marriage Register."

Drena realised with relief that he was not looking for her. "Y . . . yes, of course. I think it is in the vestry."

She moved towards the vestry which opened out of the Chancel and the newcomer asked, "Surely you are not French? How can you be anything but English?"

Drena laughed. "As it happens, I am a quarter French but I live in England."

"Then let us speak in English," the newcomer said, speaking in that language.

Because he spoke so perfectly Drena said, "And now I am certain that you too are English."

"Shall I say that I am half and half?" he replied. "And now, tell me what you are doing here."

"I am sweeping the floor," Drena replied.

"I can see that," he said, "but I did not expect to find anyone so beautiful, so fair, and so obviously English, here in this little Church in the middle of nowhere!"

"I hardly think that is complimentary to Fabrey!" Drena replied. "And you must be aware that Burgundy is the most important Province in the whole of France."

"I know that," the newcomer said, "and now I think we should introduce ourselves. Will you tell me your name?"

"My name is Drena," she replied, "and that, I assure you, is an English name."

"And I am Francis, which is also English," the newcomer replied, "and I am well aware, Miss Drena, that you are rebuking me for being too inquisitive."

Drena laughed again. "As few strangers ever come to Fabrey, you will find that people will be very curious about you too."

"And I am curious to see the Marriage Register."

"Of course," Drena said quickly, feeling she had been unnecessarily talkative. "If you will come this way, Monsieur, I will show you where it is."

She walked ahead of him down the chancel and in through the door which opened by the altar, and which led into the very small Vestry. Father Jean's surplices were hanging from a wooden peg, and here was a table on which was a pile of Registers of Births, Marriages and Deaths.

Drena looked at the first one and seeing it was for Births pushed it aside. The next she pushed towards Monsieur Francis. "I am sure you will find what you are looking for here," she said.

As she spoke she opened the book. It was very old and the entries dated back to the time the Church was built, which was at the beginning of the 18th century.

The newcomer looked carefully at the first page to ascertain the date of the first entry. Then he quickly turned over a large number of pages before slowing down. He was obviously searching for an entry in one particular later year.

He did not speak and Drena wondered, if he was going to take a long time, whether he would like a chair from the nave. Now as he was looking down she could see him very clearly and she thought he was extremely handsome. He looked very English, but there was also something about him which she felt he owed to his French ancestors.

She wondered whether it was his father or his mother who was French, but thought it would seem impertinent for her to ask.

He turned over another page, then gave an exclamation.

"What is it?" she enquired.

"There is a page missing," he said.

She then came round the table to look at the Register. "How do you know?" she enquired.

"There were no marriages registered from 1789 to 1790."

That was true, and to make sure, Drena turned back. She saw that the page before ended in 1788, which was before the Revolution. Then on the next page, they started in 1791. "Surely, there must have been some marriages in the years between?" she said.

"That is what I am thinking," Monsieur Francis replied, "and what in fact I am seeking."

"You will have to ask Father Jean what has happened to the missing pages," Drena said.

"Father Jean?" the newcomer exclaimed. "Do you mean he is still here?"

"Yes, he is here. Do you know him?"

"I know of him, and I would like to see him at once!"

"Then you will find him at the Priest's House, because he is writing his sermon for to-morrow."

The man who called himself Francis looked at her with what she thought was an expression of mock dismay. "Are you so keen to get rid of me?" he asked. "I was hoping perhaps you would be kind enough to show me the way."

"I have not yet finished my sweeping," Drena said, "but as it is nearly luncheon-time, I think perhaps I can leave it until later."

"I should be very disappointed if I had to grope my way around the village, and perhaps call at the wrong house," Monsieur Francis said.

Drena laughed. "It is not so large that you are likely to become lost," she said, "but I will take you to Father Jean."

She closed the book and put it on top of the Register of Births. Walking ahead of him she stepped out of the Church into the sunshine.

Outside the Churchyard she saw to her astonishment a very smart, impressive-looking phaeton drawn by four exceedingly fine horses. The groom in charge was wearing what she was sure was an English livery and a cockaded tall-hat.

When Monsieur Francis appeared, the groom jumped down from the phaeton and waited for his master to climb into the driving-seat.

"It is only a short distance," Drena said. "We can easily walk."

"I think I should bring my phaeton with me," Monsieur Francis replied.

As he spoke he helped Drena onto the seat beside him, so that there was no argument about it. He picked up the reins and the groom jumped into the seat behind.

Drena directed him and as they approached the small Priest's House she said, "I am sure Father Jean will ask you to stay to luncheon. What will you do about your servant?"

"He has a hamper," Monsieur Francis said, "and naturally, I have one too. I would be delighted to accept an invitation to eat comfortably inside the Priest's House, and perhaps I could offer my pâté as a contribution towards the meal."

"I can assure you it would be very much appreciated," Drena answered.

Monsieur Francis told his servant in English to give him the pâté. The man produced it from inside a luggage hamper, and with it came a bottle of champagne.

"I would not wish to be an encumbrance to my host," Monsieur Francis said with a smile.

"You will certainly not be that," Drena remarked, "with such a very generous contribution to the household."

She thought as she spoke that he was obviously a very rich man. She might, before he left, be able to persuade him to give her a contribution towards the Orphanage, but for the moment she was concerned with introducing him to Father Jean.

The newcomer put the pâté and the bottle of champagne with his hat down on the table in the hall, and Drena went ahead to the Study.

As she expected, Father Jean was writing his sermon. She knew there would be very few people in the Church to hear it, but those who could came because they loved him, and they knew he would be disappointed if they were not there.

Drena had already learned there were some people who were too old to move from their cottages, and others who were too blind or disabled to manage even the short distance to the Church. She wondered as she moved to his Study what Father Jean would make of Monsieur Francis.

She opened the door and Father Jean looked up. "It cannot yet be luncheon-time!" he said.

"It is very near it, Father," Drena replied, "but you have a visitor."

Father Jean rose to his feet and Monsieur Francis stepped forward. "I am so delighted, Father," he said, "to learn that you are still here. I have heard about you, but did not think I would be fortunate enough to find you."

"I am here, my son, and, of course, must welcome you to Fabrey."

"Thank you," Monsieur Francis said. "What I want to ask you, Father, before we go any further is what has happened to the pages of the Marriage Register which record the years 1789 to 1790?"

To Drena's surprise, she saw Father Jean stiffen. In a voice that sounded different from the way he usually spoke, he asked sharply, "Why should you want them?"

"They are very important to me," Monsieur Francis replied.

"Will you forgive me if I ask why?" Father Jean enquired.

There was a little pause.

Then Monsieur Francis said quietly, "It was then that you, Father, married my mother to my father, and that is why I want to see the entry, and it is of the utmost importance that I should."

CHAPTER SIX

There was silence. The Priest did not speak, and eventually Monsieur Francis said, "I think I had better tell you what happened, and you will understand why I am so anxious to see the record of the Marriage.

The Priest indicated with his hand two chairs in front of the desk and both Drena and Monsieur Francis sat down.

She was looking at him as she waited for him to speak and thought again that he was undoubtedly extremely handsome. But she still had the feeling that she had when he had first arrived that she had seen him before.

Slowly, in a deep, quiet voice, Monsieur Francis began. "When the Duchesse Alise was living here in the Château, she had been joined by a young girl called Yvette who was a distant relation. She was a member of a distinguished family who were, however, not well off. Yvette came to the Duchesse to be her reader as she was becoming too blind to read clearly for herself."

Father Jean nodded as if he remembered that.

"When the first news of the Revolution came to Burgundy," Monsieur Francis went on: "it was thought that it would not extend beyond Paris, but as the year 1789 passed there was news that revolutionary activities were breaking out in many other parts of France."

"That is true," Father Jean murmured. "It did not however affect anyone considerably in Fabrey, and we thought the disturbances would soon be over."

"Early in the following year, however, the Revolutionaries in Dijon stormed the Palace of the Ducs," Monsieur Francis went on, "doing a great deal of damage to the interior of the great Palace."

"I remember that is what happened," Father Jean affirmed, "and I was deeply perturbed about it at the time."

"So also was the Duc of Saulieu," Monsieur Francis said. "As things were getting uncomfortable and it seemed as if the Revolutionaries might attack the Château in Saulieu, he came to Fabrey to see his mother."

"I remember his coming," Father Jean said. "There was never a finer or more noble man."

"That is what I have always heard about him," Monsieur Francis said. "When he had visited the Duchesse Alise on a previous occasion, he had met Yvette, and found her very attractive."

Listening, Drena was suddenly alert. It had been assumed that the Duc François had died unmarried, but yet it seemed that Monsieur Francis's tale might assert the contrary.

"The Duc came," Monsieur Francis continued, "because he had learned of the disturbances in Dijon and was worried about his Mother. Sadly the very night he arrived, she died."

"I recall it very vividly," Father Jean murmured.

"The Duc, I think, was glad that he was with his Mother, of whom he was very fond, when she departed this life," Monsieur Francis said. "Because he was worried about the course of the Revolution, he arranged with you, Father Jean, that she should be buried immediately."

"That is true," Father Jean averred. "And the whole village wept because the Duchesse had left them. She had been very kind to the old people, and everyone respected and loved her."

He spoke very movingly.

Monsieur Francis was silent for some moments before he continued, "The Duc was now very worried as to what would happen to Yvette. She was only eighteen and her family lived a long way away."

He smiled before he went on, "I think you will remember, Father, what happened. He married Yvette, and knew she was the woman he had been looking for all his life."

"She was very beautiful," Father Jean said, "and the Duc was the most handsome man I have ever seen. They made a perfect couple, and I married them in the Chapel early in the morning, the day after the Duchesse Alise was buried.

"They stayed here in the Château," Monsieur Francis continued, "and had nearly a week of blissful happiness together. Then the blow fell."

"You mean," Drena chimed in, as if she could not prevent herself, "that the Revolutionaries came here."

"They came in search of the Duc François," Monsieur Francis replied, "having failed to find him in the Château at Saulieu."

"What . . . happened?" Drena asked. She knew the answer, and felt she could not bear to hear it.

"When the Duc realised they were outside the Château," Monsieur Francis replied, "he hid Yvette in a secret cupboard, making her lock herself in."

"'You must not come out, my darling,' he said, 'until they have gone. Then I am sure Father Jean will find some way of helping you to reach your family.'

"She sighed and clung to him, begging him to hide with her, but he was determined that she should not be in any danger. When the Revolutionaries came to the door of the Château, he went out and gave himself up to them."

"How could he do anything so brave?" Drena asked.

"He was too proud not to face his enemies," Monsieur Francis replied, "he also hoped that if they made him their prisoner, they would not search the Château for anyone else."

"So they ... took him ... away," Drena said in a whisper.

"They took him to Dijon, and guillotined him after a trial that was nothing more than a mockery!"

Monsieur Francis's voice was harsh and the old Priest shook his head sadly as he said, "It was cruel and wicked, for Duc François would have looked after his people, as the present Duc has failed to do."

"That is what I have heard," Monsieur Francis answered, "but I have not yet finished my story."

"Then please go on," Father Jean begged. "I have often wondered what became of Yvette after she left here."

"You will remember," Monsieur Francis said, "that quite unexpectedly an Englishman appeared. He was in the Diplomatic Corps and had met Yvette when he was in France the previous year. When he learned how shockingly the Revolutionaries were behaving, he came from Florence, where he was on the Ambassador's staff, because he knew he must save her."

"He thought she ... too might ... be guillotined?" Drena asked.

"She came from a distinguished family and was a relative of the Duchesse Alise, and that was enough to sign her death warrant!"

"It is ... frightening to ... think ... about!" Drena exclaimed in horror.

"Fortunately her friend from the British Diplomatic Corps was determined to save her. He arrived here on the very day she emerged from her hiding-place and took her to the South of France where he asked her to marry him."

He paused for breath before he went on, "She was aware that he had come to save her because he was already in love with her, and since she had just realised that she was expecting a baby, she accepted his proposal."

"She was having a ... baby?" Father Jean exclaimed. "Then it was ... the child ..."

"... of Duc François," Monsieur Francis finished quietly.

"But ... no one ever ... knew he was ... married," Drena remarked. "His portrait hangs in the Château at Saulieu and the Curator said how sad it was that he never married."

"No one knew he had married Yvette," Monsieur Francis said, "nor did her English husband. She kept silent because she was afraid that her child might be in danger, as well as herself."

"B ... but ... the child ...?" Drena murmured.

"He was brought up as Lord Lamdon's son, and when his supposed father died he inherited the title."

Monsieur Francis was still speaking very quietly.

Drena stared at him, then suddenly she exclaimed, "It was ... you! You are ... the son of Duc François! I know now where I have seen you before! You resemble so closely the portrait of your father that hangs in the Château over the mantelpiece in the Library!"

Monsieur Francis smiled. "It was only very shortly

before my Mother died that she told me that I looked very like my father and who, in fact, my father really was."

"But, why . . . why did she . . . keep it a secret?"

"Because Lord Lamdon was very much older than her and she was not able to have another child. He was very proud of the boy he thought was his, and it would have been extremely cruel and unkind to tell him that she had deceived him."

He paused before he said, "Only after I had inherited his title did she tell me the truth, and that was when she knew that she herself had only a short time to live."

He looked at the Priest before he said, "And that is why, Father Jean, I have come here to confirm what my mother told me by asking to see the official record of her Marriage."

"It is quite safe, I can assure you," Father Jean answered. "I deliberately removed it from the Register for fear the Revolutionaries would see it and try to find and execute Yvette because the Duc François had made her the Duchesse de Saulieu."

"That was very sensible of you!"

"I have it here," Father Jean went on.

He pulled out a drawer of his writing-desk as he spoke and took from it the missing page of the Register.

He passed it to Monsieur Francis who took it eagerly from him.

"I see they were married on the 20th May 1790," he said quietly, "and I was born in March 1791."

"And we know now that as Duc François's son, you are the rightful Duc of Saulieu!"

Father Jean spoke almost as if he was making a proclamation.

"You have confirmed exactly what my mother told me," Monsieur Francis said, "but you will understand, Father, that having been brought up by an Englishman in England and having eventually inherited his title, it is going to be very hard for me to know what I should do."

He paused and then said, "Meanwhile, I suggest that you think of me and address me simply as Francis."

As he spoke he looked at Drena and she said quickly, "But you are needed in France! You are needed ... desperately! The present Duc is cruel! Wicked! He is prepared even to stoop to murder!"

Francis stiffened. Then he asked sharply, "What do you mean by that?"

"I think I must explain first that I am the daughter of the Earl of Winterton, and his father married Aimée, a daughter of the then Duc of Saulieu."

She paused and then continued, "She, my Grandmother, now the Dowager Countess, is a very rich woman in her own right and has made me her heiress."

Drena paused to give them time to absorb this remarkable information. "We are both now guests of Duc Roger," she went on, "but I have come here to seek sanctuary. I overheard through one of the listening-holes in the Château, the Duc telling his mistress that he intended to marry me so that he would get control of my money."

She sighed and then said, "Immediately afterwards he planned to murder both my Grandmother and me, so that my fortune would then be his to spend not in Burgundy but in Paris!"

Both Francis and Father Jean stared at her as if they could not believe what they were hearing. Then the Priest said, "Is this really true, my child?"

"I swear to you, Father, it is the truth, exactly as I heard it, and that is why I ran away. I am waiting now to hear from my father's Solicitor, whom I can trust, to come to me from England."

She gave what was almost a little sob before she said, "The Duc was planning, if I refused to marry him, to drug me so that I would feebly acquiesce when he insisted that our marriage should take place immediately."

"How can any man behave in such a monstrous fashion?" Francis asked angrily.

"You should see the way he has neglected his estate," Drena said. "He is not in the least interested in it. His people are half-starved, there is no money for the orphans here who are housed in the Duchesse Alise's Château, and the same applies to everything at Saulieu."

"So you think," Francis said gently, "that I ought to try to put things to rights?"

"It is your duty to do so. If your mother could be brave enough to save you by taking you out of France, surely you must now come back to save your people!

They are suffering at the hands of a man who is a monster and unworthy of the title which has always been revered in Burgundy."

Francis was listening, and now he looked at Father Jean. "And what do you tell me to do, Father?"

"I think, my son," the Priest replied, "you must listen to your heart and your soul. They will guide you to do what is right in the eyes of God."

"Then I will go to Saulieu," Francis said. "But first, Father, as I have travelled quite a long way, I would like, if it is possible, to stay the night in Fabrey."

The old Priest nodded. "Of course you must do that, and although it may not be very comfortable, I welcome you warmly to my house."

"Thank you," Francis murmured.

"There is one thing I cannot do," the Priest went on, "and that is to stable your horses. But Drena will take you to the stables at the Château, where there is plenty of room for them."

"I will take you," Drena said, "and I am sure you would like to see where the Duchesse Alise and your mother once lived."

"Of course I would," Francis said.

He picked up the page from the Marriage Register from the desk saying, "You will understand, Father, that I will need this with me. I cannot believe that the present Duc will accept what I have to say without a great deal of argument and bluster."

"That is certainly true," Father Jean agreed. "But the family have only to look at you to know how strongly you resemble your father."

"I was christened after him," Francis said, "but my mother naturally gave me the English version of his name."

"Well, now you can be 'François'," Drena exclaimed, "and another Duc François is exactly what Saulieu needs desperately!"

Francis smiled back at her.

He put the page of the Marriage Register down again on the table saying, "I think, Father, I will leave this with you while I stable my horses." He and Drena then went outside to where his team was waiting.

For the rest of the day everything seemed like a dream. To Drena every minute was a delight as François, as she now called him, told her of his life in England. He explained how he had been brought up in the same way as any English boy, going first to Eton and then to Oxford, as Lord Lamdon had done before him.

He had travelled to various places abroad where the man he had called his father was posted as a diplomat. He had lived in St. Petersburg before Napoleon Bonaparte had attacked the Russians, and after that in Washington in America.

There Lord Lamdon had been a very effective and admired Ambassador for Britain.

"When he retired," François said, "my mother and I returned with him to England, where on his death he left me a very attractive house in Buckinghamshire. It has however with it only a small estate. I joined the Household Cavalry, but by then the war with France had nearly ended."

"Surely your mother was distressed that Britain was at war with her country?" Drena asked.

"I did not realise until after my 'father' died how much it must have hurt her, and how unhappy she was for the people to whom she belonged."

"That is why you must come back and put things to rights," Drena said.

There was a little silence before François asked unexpectedly.

"And are you prepared to help me?"

"I will try to," Drena answered, "but do you mean you want me to go back to Saulieu with you?"

"You ran away, as you told me, because you were afraid you would have to marry the Duc. I promise you that will not happen, and it will be easier for the man you have asked to come from London to deal with him at Saulieu than here."

"Yes . . . of course," Drena said, "and the Duc can no longer make me marry him, if he is no longer the Duc!"

She felt a feeling of relief seep through her. It was as if a cloud that had obscured the sun had been swept away.

After they had had a simple evening meal at the Priest's House, Father Jean left them alone in the Sitting Room, saying he had not yet finished writing his sermon.

When they were alone Drena said, "What are you planning to do tomorrow when you reach the Château de Saulieu? Are you certain you are strong enough to confront Duc Roger without anyone to protect you?"

"I have two outriders with me," François replied. "I thought it would be a mistake to bring them with me into Fabrey, and draw attention to myself. They are waiting for me at an Inn about a mile away. We will collect them on the way tomorrow."

Drena smiled. "I can see you are very practical, which is exactly how I would expect an Englishman to be in a situation like this!"

"I think from all you have told me that we are very much alike," Francois said. "Your Father was half-French and therefore your French blood responds to all that is beautiful in France. And although by blood I am wholly French, my upbringing literally from the cradle has been entirely English."

"In which case," Drena laughed, "we should represent both countries extremely well."

"I hope that is what I can do," François said, "but, as you have already told me, it will not be easy."

They talked until after midnight, and when Drena went to bed she prayed that he would be able without too much unpleasantness to supplant Duc Roger. Then Saulieu would be free of him for ever.

She gathered from what François told her that he was very rich. That meant he would perhaps be able to make Roger an ample allowance as long as he behaved himself. Yet at the same time she was afraid.

Roger de Saulieu had frightened her so terribly that she had run away from the Château. She could not help feeling she was going back into what the young Englishman who had warned her about him would call the "Lion's Den".

"I must help François", she whispered.

Then she was praying. "Please, God, protect him. Please do not let him be murdered, which I am sure Duc Roger will try to do."

It was a prayer that came from the very depths of her heart.

She went on praying until she fell asleep.

The next morning the horses were waiting for them outside the Priest's house after they had finished breakfast.

Because she was going back to her Grandmother, Drena had already given all the money she had left to Madame Muate.

"This is for you and Father Jean," she said, "and also for the orphans. I will send you some more as soon as I arrive in Saulieu, and I promise you there will be money coming to you regularly when I return to England."

She was certain she could arrange with her Grandmother to do this when the Dowager Countess learned how much it was needed in the village where the Duchesse Alise had lived.

Madame Muate had looked almost tearfully at the number of francs which Drena handed her. "You are too generous!" she cried. "I have lain awake night after night worrying about money, and now you have given me this!"

Drena put her arms round her and kissed her. "You will never have to worry like that again," she said. "I promise you, I will always help you and I know that now the Duc François is with us, everything will be different."

Madame Muate had been told by Father Jean who 'Monsieur' François really was. When she took him his breakfast she had curtsied before she put the plate down on the table.

He had smiled and said, "You are going too fast, Madame. I am still not a Duc until I have been accepted by my own people."

"To me, Monsieur," Madame replied, "you are a Messenger from God, and who could ask for more?"

"Who indeed?" François replied, but his eyes were twinkling.

Drena kissed Madame Muate and Father Jean goodbye. "Thank you very much for having me," she said, "and I promise you I shall come back whenever it is possible for me to do so."

"You must come," Madame Muate said, "because we need you and love you. You have brought us a great deal of happiness, and now everything will be changed for the better."

The old Priest blessed them. As they drove away Drena said, "He is very old. You must go back and see him as soon as it is possible for you to do so."

"I have left him money for the orphans and for the restoration of the Church," François replied.

"I thought you would," Drena said, "and I gave Madame Muate what money I had left for food. That, to my mind, is more important than anything else."

"Of course you are right," François agreed. "Is that the English or the French part of you?"

He was teasing her and Drena laughed. "I hope it is both," she said. "I love France, just as I thought I would when I heard about it, read about it and dreamt of it ever since I was a child."

"I wish I could say the same," François remarked. "But I know now that my mother and father bred in me something that responds to everything I see, every word I hear. I had always believed that my thoughts were very English. But now I know that I am completely and absolutely French."

The way he spoke was very moving, and Drena felt he was dedicating himself to the task that lay ahead of him. She was well aware that his confrontation with Duc Roger would be a very difficult one.

The team of horses swallowed up the miles and they reached Saulieu in half the time it had taken Drena to ride to Fabrey. As they drew near to the Château which looked exquisitely beautiful in the sunshine, Drena heard François draw in his breath. As they entered the courtyard, François gasped in astonishment.

They had picked up the outriders on the way. Now, as they dismounted from their horses and François drew the phaeton to a standstill, the servants waiting at the door stared at them in amazement.

Drena had sent another letter to Sir Matthew saying that she was going back to the Château at Saulieu. She had also asked Father Jean to send him there as quickly as possible if he arrived in Fabrey.

Despite the fact that François was with her together

with three of his servants, Drena's heart was pounding with fear as they entered the Great Hall.

"Where is Madame la Comtesse?" Drena asked, to be told that she was in the Salon with Monsieur le Duc.

She knew as she followed the old servant who opened the door for them that her heart was fluttering. The servant announced her.

"M'Lady Drena!"

As he spoke, the Duc, who was sitting with her Grandmother by the fireside, sprang to his feet.

"You are back!" he exclaimed angrily. "How could you have frightened us all by disappearing in that mysterious manner?"

"I am back, Grandmama," Drena said, "and I have brought with me somebody I particularly want you to meet."

"I was so worried about you, ma chérie," the Dowager Countess said.

Then as she looked at François there was a puzzled expression in her old eyes.

"May I present you, Grandmama," Drena said, "to the Duc François of Saulieu!"

CHAPTER SEVEN

"Do you really expect me to believe this absurd nonsense?" Duc Roger asked angrily.

His voice seemed to echo round the Salon.

"The Mayor of Dijon and Judge Lassuls, the Supreme High Court Judge of Burgundy, both found it completely credible," Francois replied. "I called at the Palace of the Ducs and States of Burgundy before I went to Fabrey."

He paused for a moment then went on. "When they saw me they both exclaimed that I was exactly like my father, whom they had known. I left with them my Birth Certificate and promised them that they should have the entry in the Marriage Register as soon as I could obtain it. It is being taken to them now by one of my servants."

François spoke in a slow, quiet voice, and Drena realised that everyone was impressed except Roger.

The Dowager Countess exclaimed before anyone else spoke, "But of course, no one could dispute that you are Duc François' son! You are exactly like him! I thought when you walked into the room I was seeing a ghost!"

Duc Roger looked at her with a furious expression in his eyes.

The two elderly relatives who were sitting with him and the Dowager Countess when they arrived affirmed that he was the living image of Duc François.

Drena and François had arrived at the Château soon after two o'clock, although they had stopped on the way for luncheon, but the horses had moved very swiftly. She assumed that Duc Roger would have luncheon as usual at one o'clock, which meant that he and his guests would only just have moved from the Dining Hall into the Salon.

Now they were all seated, except for François, who was telling his story in the same way that he had told it to her.

Drena, watching him, could see how calm and composed he was. At the same time she knew that Duc Roger was becoming more and more furious as the tale unfolded.

When François revealed that he had already been to the Palace of the Ducs he said, "Are you seriously intending to pursue this very dubious claim of being the Duc de Saulieu?"

"I think I am needed here," François said quietly.

"He is also needed in Fabrey," Drena added. "The Orphanage has been housed in the Duchesse Alise's

Château, but they are so pressed for money that the children are on the verge of starvation and the people in the village stay alive only on what they can grow in their gardens."

"You can hardly say that is my fault!" Duc Roger stormed. "I have not enough money for myself, let alone for a lot of ne'er-do-wells who should work and have their earnings to spend."

"This sort of conversation will get us nowhere," François said quietly. "What I am asking is that I may stay here in the Château while we work out some plan for the future."

He looked at Duc Roger and when he did not reply went on, "I have also asked the Mayor of Dijon if he will send one of his most highly qualified Lawyers to look into the finances of the Duc of Saulieu, whoever he may be, and see how much we can apportion to the family and to those who look to us for our protection and support."

The way he spoke was very impressive, but Duc Roger merely snarled, "Taking a lot upon yourself, are you not? Well, I have a great deal to say where that is concerned."

"Of course," François agreed, "and it is only fair that you should have your appropriate share of what is available."

"And that will be precious little – I can tell you." Roger retorted.

As he spoke the door opened and the Comtesse de Pastel came in. She stared first at Drena, and said in a hostile voice, "So you have returned have you?

How could you have been so inconsiderate as not to let your Grandmother and the Duc know where you were staying?"

"That is not important at the moment," Roger interrupted. "This man who Drena has brought back with her claims to be the rightful Duc de Saulieu. So it looks as if I am to be turned out into the gutter!"

Eugénie Pastel looked at Roger in disbelief. "The rightful Duc de Saulieu?" she exclaimed. "How can that be possible?"

"I am sure that Roger de Saulieu can explain that to you in detail," François replied. "I suggest that, while he does so, Drena and I and her Grandmother move into another room or into the garden. I am sure Roger de Saulieu will wish to discuss the situation with you privately."

Nobody replied and he walked towards the French window which opened out into the garden.

Drena followed him. After a moment the Dowager Countess rose to her feet. As soon as they were outside Drena could hear Roger's voice rising in fury as he told the Comtesse his version of the situation.

They walked across the lawn until they came to some seats in the shade of a large tree.

It was then the Dowager Countess said to François, "You must tell me again, dear boy, about your mother and her marriage to François. He was one of the most attractive men I have ever met, and I have always thought what a disaster it was for the family that he lost his life on the guillotine."

"I wish I had known him," François said. "My mother often spoke of him when she talked about the family, and I grew up thinking he was a hero even though I had no idea he was my real father."

"You are so exactly like him," the Dowager Countess said, "that it is quite uncanny!"

"I only hope I can be like him in caring for our people," François answered, "and doing what is right and just where the family is concerned."

The Dowager Countess did not stay with them long, but went back into the Château. "I am going to rest," she said, "because I feel there will be more discussions later in the day at which I should be present."

François escorted her politely to a side-door, knowing she would not want to go back into the Salon.

When he rejoined Drena he said, "I am very sorry that you should be involved in all this. It is unpleasant for you, and I only hope we can settle things amicably when the Lawyers arrive from Dijon."

"I . . . I thought . . . perhaps," Drena said hesitatingly, "you could . . . give Duc Roger an allowance . . . which will enable him to . . . live in Paris in . . . comfort."

"I have every intention of doing that," François replied, "and fortunately, whether I am a Duc or a Lord, I am a very rich man!"

"That will certainly please Duc Roger," Drena said. "I do not think he has any real interest in his position here, or in the people who have relied on the Saulieus for centuries."

"It is very sad that they should suffer so much," François said, "but I feel we can make things very different in the future."

"*We?*" Drena queried in a small voice.

"That is something I want to talk to you about," François answered. "As soon as things are more settled, and I know whether I am in the future to stay here, or return to England."

"But you . . . must stay here . . . you must . . . help the people," Drena cried.

She paused for a moment before she went on:

"I wish you could have seen the orphans' faces when, thanks to the money I had given to Mademoiselle Alesia, they had a proper meal for the first time for weeks! Their delight was something I shall never forget, and I intend to send regular amounts of money for them, wherever I may be."

"I think what they want from you is more than money," François said.

Drena thought innocently that he was referring to the stories she told them.

"If I cannot be in the Orphanage myself," she said, "I will try to find somebody to help Mademoiselle Alesia, who will not only amuse the children, but also educate them."

"I agree with you, that is important," François said.

Drena however had the feeling that he was thinking of something different.

They sat talking for well over an hour, then as no one came near them, they walked in the shade of the trees to look at other parts of the garden, where it was obvious there was a shortage of gardeners. At the same time, the flowers were still beautiful and there were shrubs in blossom, which gave out a fragrance that scented the air.

They had walked some little way from the house when suddenly a small boy appeared, running so swiftly towards them that he was breathless.

"My little sister – my little sister!" he cried. "She has fallen into the lake!"

Both Drena and François stiffened.

"Come quickly! Help! Help!" the boy gasped.

Drena knew where the lake was, although she had not been particularly interested in it. There had been so many other things to see, but now she started to run to where it lay behind the Château, down a steep grassy slope.

It was a very pretty lake with irises in bloom on either side of it, and it widened into being quite broad at the point they reached first. They stared down into the water which glimmered in the sunshine, but there was no sign of any small child.

"Show me where your sister fell in," François said, turning towards the boy.

As he spoke, both he and Drena were aware that the little boy was no longer with them. When they had run hastily in the direction of the lake, he might have gone into the house perhaps to find more people to help rescue his sister.

"Where can the child be?" Drena asked anxiously.

François put his hand over his eyes to shield them

from the glare of the sun that came from the water.

He looked first one way, then the other.

Drena was doing the same thing. Then a bee came buzzing near her face and she turned her head to shoo it away. As she did so she screamed, and it saved her life.

For coming down the slope behind them were two horses moving at a tremendous speed, and driven by Roger who was standing up in a heavy open farm-cart with large wheels.

As François turned, alerted by Drena's scream, he saw the approaching cart bearing down on them.

He literally threw her to one side and fell on top of her. As he did so, the horses passed them with barely an inch to spare.

Just before they reached the lake, Roger, throwing down the reins, jumped. But he caught his foot in a trace, and instead of landing safely on the grass he fell, still attached to the vehicle.

A back wheel of the cart ran right over his head.

The horses tried to prevent themselves from galloping straight into the water, but the weight of the vehicle behind them was too heavy. There was a tremendous splash, and the water sprayed high into the air spattering Drena and François where they lay.

Drena managed to sit up and wipe the water from her eyes, and realised that François was doing the same.

Then they saw in front of them the back of the cart sinking slowly until it disappeared, without sign of Roger or the horses.

Hardly realising what they were doing, Drena and François rose to their feet.

As the full horror of what had occurred swept over her Drena flung herself against François crying, "He was . . . trying to . . . k . . . kill . . . you! He was . . . trying to . . . kill . . . you!"

"And you!" François replied.

Then his arms were round her and his lips were on hers. He kissed her fiercely, almost violently, as if he thought he might have lost her.

For the moment she could not believe it was happening. Then as a shaft of sunlight seemed to seep through her body she felt a wild rapture she had never known.

François drew her closer and his lips became a little more gentle. At the same time they were very possessive. It was then that Drena knew this was love, and she had in fact loved him ever since she had first seen him.

She felt as if her whole body melted into his and they were a part of each other. François kissed her and went on kissing her until the sunshine seemed to envelop them both. For Drena the intensity and ecstasy were almost too much to bear. She gave a little murmur and hid her face against his neck.

"My darling, my sweet!" François said. "I might have lost you!"

"H . . . he meant to . . . k . . . kill . . . you!" Drena whispered.

"I know that," François said, "but instead he has destroyed himself."

Because she could hardly believe it, Drena moved so that she could look into the lake. There was not a sign that anything had happened. The water was still and clear as it had been when they first arrived there.

"He is dead," François said quietly, "and I do not believe that anyone will mourn him."

"But . . . you are . . . alive!" Drena murmured.

"And so are you, my lovely one," François replied. "How soon will you marry me? Because I cannot live without you."

Suddenly Drena felt shy, and she hid her face once more against his neck.

"I have loved you since the first moment I saw you," François said. "When I went into that little Church, I thought you were an Angel who was brushing away so diligently."

"And I . . . thought I had . . . seen you before, but I could not . . . think where."

"I think we have both lived before, and loved before," François said, "because I was aware when we talked that you were everything I had been looking for all my life."

"Is that . . . really true?" Drena asked.

"Do you think I would lie to you about anything so sacred as our love?" François asked.

"Oh . . . François . . .! I do love you," Drena said, "but . . . because I had never . . . been in love before, I did not . . . understand until you . . . kissed me what I was . . . feeling except that it was . . . wonderful . . . so absolutely perfect!"

"And that is how it will always be," François promised. "So, my darling, answer my question – how soon will you marry me?"

"Now . . . this moment . . . at once!" Drena cried.

He gave a laugh that was one of sheer triumph.

"That is what I wanted you to say," he smiled.

Then he was kissing her again, and it seemed as if a century passed before they reluctantly went back to the Château.

"You will have to tell . . . everyone what . . . has happened," Drena said. "And what about the little boy?"

"I think he was paid by Roger to make us go to the lake," François replied.

"You mean he did not have a sister?" Drena asked.

"Forget it," François said. "We must try not to think of what happened because God has saved us."

Drena thought as he spoke that it seemed for the moment unimportant. She loved François and for her everything else did not matter.

"You will have to tell everyone," she murmured again.

"I will do that," François said quietly. "But I think, my darling, you have been through enough drama for the moment, so I suggest you go and find your Grandmother and stay with her until all the unpleasantness is over."

Drena slipped her hand into his. "You are quite certain you can manage without me?"

She was only teasing him and his fingers tightened on hers.

"I could never manage without you, my adorable one," he said, "but I want to protect you from everything that is ugly and unpleasant." He paused for a moment, then continued smiling at her, "You are so beautiful that I want to put you in a glass case and just worship you!"

Drena felt herself quiver at the sincerity in his voice. "I just ... want to be ... with you," she whispered.

"And that is exactly what you will be," François promised.

They reached the Château and François deliberately took Drena in through the front door. There was no one in the hall and he stopped at the bottom of the stairs. "I will join you as soon as I can," he said quietly as he raised her hand to his lips.

Because she knew it was what he wanted, she ran up the stairs quickly. She knew that as soon as she was out of sight François would alert the servants as to what had happened. He would also inform the relatives who were staying in the Château that Roger was dead.

Drena went to her Grandmother's room where the Dowager Countess was reclining on a *chaise longue* in the window.

When Drena entered she held out her hand. "I have been wanting to see you, my dearest," she said. "I am so glad you are back."

Drena crossed the room to kneel beside her Grandmother. "I have some dreadful news to tell you, Grandmama," she said breathlessly.

As she explained what had happened, the Dowager Countess did not speak, but only listened with her eyes on Drena's face.

Drena told her not only how Roger had died, but also why she had left when she learned that he intended to kill them both. He would then have obtained her Grandmother's money to spend on the Comtesse. When she finished the whole sad story, Drena said, "François loves me and has asked me to . . . marry him."

It was then the Dowager Countess gave a little cry. "My dear child, my precious Granddaughter! That is what I wanted to hear!"

She smiled before she said, "I brought you here to marry the Duc de Saulieu, and that is exactly what you are going to do!"

"I am so very happy, Grandmama."

The Dowager Countess touched her face very gently. "You must forgive me for being an old fool," she said, "and not realising how bad and wicked Roger was! When you left and I saw how he was behaving with the Comtesse Eugénie, I became more and more suspicious of him."

She gave a deep sigh. "But even then," she continued, "I did not think he could stoop to murder to get the money he wanted, or that he would try to destroy François whom I know now to be as good and fine as his father was."

"I was afraid of Roger from the first minute I walked into the Château," Drena said, "but now . . . it is all over."

There was a little break in her voice and her Grandmother stroked her hair very gently. "You have to forgive me for being so blind," she said, "and also for thinking that to be a Duchess was enough to make you happy."

"I would marry François if he was as poor as Father Jean," Drena said, "and had nothing to offer me except himself."

"God has been very kind to us both," the Dowager Countess said. "Now, my dearest child, you will have everything I have always wanted for you, and more!"

"I shall have François," Drena said softly.

It was some time later that François joined them.

He knocked on the door and when the Dowager Countess told him to enter he came in.

Drena, who was still sitting on the floor at her Grandmother's feet, jumped up. She was so pleased to see him that she ran towards him and he put his arms around her.

"It is over, my darling," he said, "and now we can plan our future, with, I hope, your Grandmother's blessing."

He looked at the Dowager Countess as he spoke, and she held out her hand.

"Drena has told me everything," she said, "and I am so very, very grateful to you for saving her life. Now there are no more difficulties about your taking your rightful place as the Duc de Saulieu."

"It is something I am only too willing to do," François said, "as long as I have your permission to marry Drena immediately."

"I have no objection," the Dowager Countess answered, "and I am sure Drena's father will agree when I tell him why it was important."

François smiled at her. "As I anticipated that would

be your reply, I have already sent for Father Antion, who I understand is my Private Chaplain."

"You intend to be married at once?" the Dowager Countess asked.

"Because we will be in mourning, and also because I know there are a great many things to discuss, to change and improve upon," François said. "I want tonight to think only of my happiness and of Drena's. We will therefore be married very quietly immediately after dinner, and the only person left in the house then will be yourself."

"As I am here, I hope I may stay," the Dowager Countess said.

"But of course," François replied, "and I can never thank you enough for bringing Drena to France. If you had not done so, we might never have found each other, and I would have remained a man lost because he was without the other half of himself."

"But we have found each other!" Drena exclaimed. "I have always felt that somewhere in the world, although I had no idea where, you were waiting for me."

"I was," François replied, "and it was fate, or rather our Guardian Angels, who brought us together in such an unlikely place."

Drena laughed and explained to her Grandmother, "I was brushing out the church in Fabrey, wearing an ugly overall belonging to Father Jean's Housekeeper, and looking not in the least like an Angel!"

"You did look like an Angel," François said firmly, "and that is how you will always look to me."

Their eyes met.

The Dowager Countess could see how close they were to each other, and sensed the rapture within them both.

She told herself that God had been very kind.

She had made a mistake in thinking that her beloved grandchild should marry Roger, the Duc de Saulieu, whatever kind of man he was.

Now it had all been put right by God himself.

Later that evening, Drena and François were married in the Private Chapel of the Château.

The Dowager Countess, watching, thought that no ceremony, however grand and important, could have been more beautiful or more moving.

Despite the shortness of time, François had managed to have the altar decorated with flowers, and there were also great vases of them standing in the Chancel.

His Private Chaplain had been told that while François had been brought up a Protestant, he had been baptised secretly in a Catholic Church. This had enabled him to have the full Marriage Service.

When finally they knelt for the blessing the Dowager Countess's eyes were filled with tears. The radiance in Drena's face was very beautiful, and she could understand why François seemed spellbound when he looked at her.

When the Chaplain had pronounced them man and wife, François kissed his Bride very gently.

It was not a kiss of passion, but of dedication to a love that was entirely spiritual.

When they went from the Chapel they did not speak to anyone, but went straight upstairs. They went first to the boudoir which was attached to the Master Bedroom. It fortunately still contained some of the priceless furniture that had been collected over the centuries by each succeeding Duc of Saulieu. The Duc closed the door behind them. "My darling, my precious, my wife!" he murmured. "You have been through so much, but now you are mine, and nothing shall ever harm you again."

"I was thanking God as we were being married," Drena said, "that I can help you in the great task that lies before you, and no one but you, François, can bring your people not only peace, but also prosperity."

"That is what I intend them to have," he said, "but you know I cannot do it without your help and inspiration, and, of course, your love."

He took her into his arms and kissed her.

At first gently, as if a feeling of sanctity was still with him. Then as her lips were soft and gentle against his, his kiss became more passionate and demanding.

François raised his head. "I thought we should have a glass of champagne so that we can toast each other," he said, "but now I want you close to me. I want to teach you, my darling, to love me as I love you."

There was no need for words.

They moved from the boudoir into the bedroom.

Again there were flowers and the scent of them filled the air.

*

A long time later, Drena moved against François' shoulder and whispered, "Is it . . . possible to be so . . . happy and . . . still be on earth?"

"The Heaven we have just found together is always there, waiting for us," François answered.

"That is what I . . . believe," Drena said, "Oh . . . darling François . . . I love you . . . I love you . . . so much!"

"And I worship and adore you," he said. "You are just perfect! How can I have been so lucky as to find you? And now that I have found you, I will never lose you!"

She knew he was thinking of how Roger might have killed her before she discovered what he intended.

She gave a little shiver and François said "Nothing like that will ever happen again, and I believe too that there will be no more Revolutions in France, certainly not in Burgundy."

"You will make sure of that!" Drena said confidently. "And your people will love you too much to allow anyone to hurt you."

"Or you."

Then he was kissing her again; kissing her demanding, as he had done before.

She felt herself melt against him until they were one person; complete in their hearts, their minds and their souls.

In the future they would be guided by love and inspired by love.

Love would envelop them from now until eternity.